Carousel

Jennifer Renson

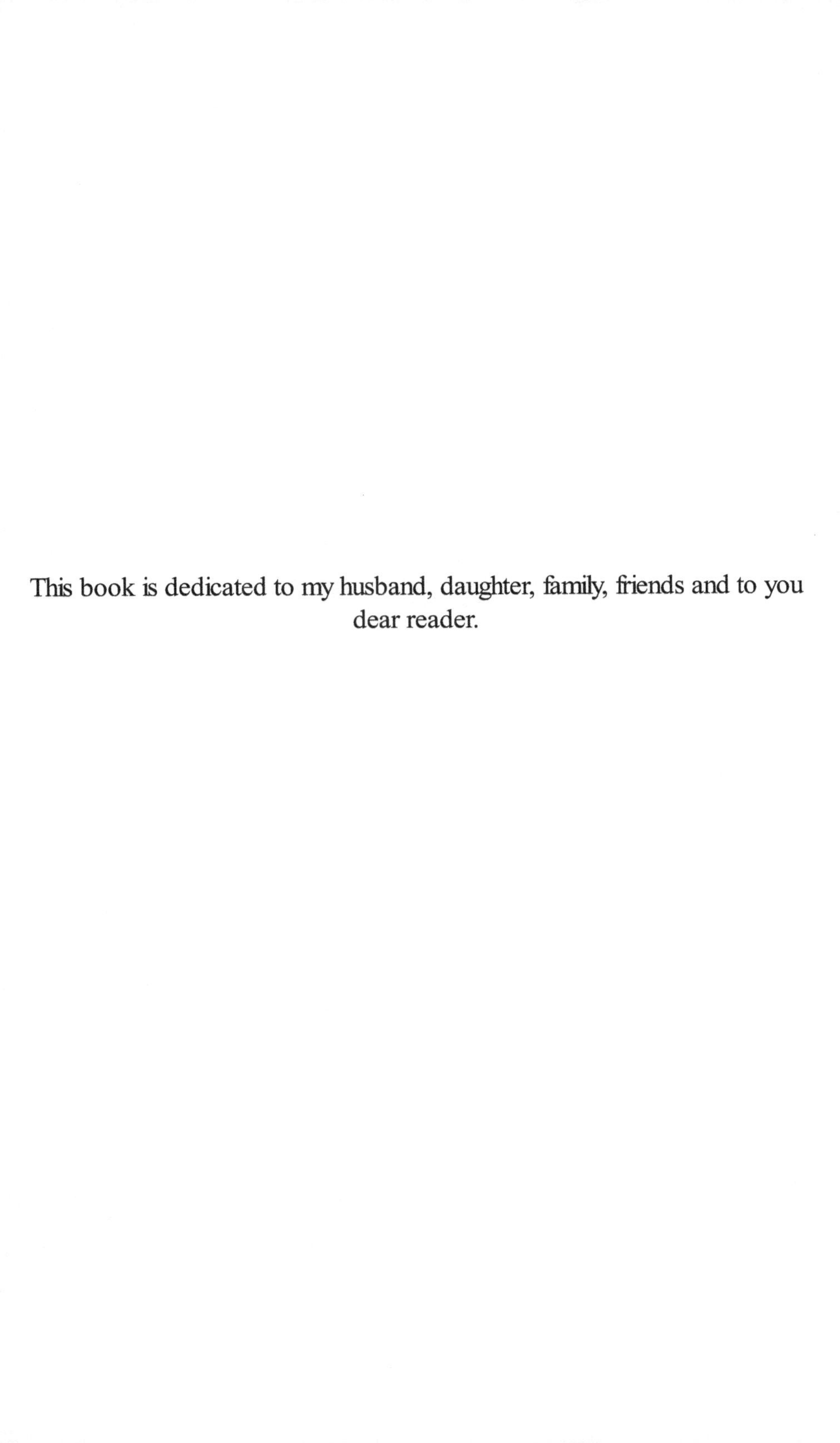

This book is dedicated to my husband, daughter, family, friends and to you dear reader.

Prologue

There once was a king and queen who ruled the tiny but prosperous kingdom of Lucca, which was north of Rome. Being well hidden from the rest of the world, the kingdom thrived in peace. The king and queen ruled over their people with a firm but gentle hand. In turn, their people adored them. For several generations, the royal family and their court lived within the palace walls, set apart from the rest of the kingdom. The families of the royal court believed they were blessed to live in such luxury behind the walls, enjoying the gardens, elaborate statues, and flower covered swings all to themselves. They were unconcerned with the lives of the common people, who were forbidden to enter the palace gates. Within the palace, they indulged their wealth and comfort, constantly throwing parties and feasting upon decadent foods.

When the king and queen were blessed with a son, a magnificent carousel was sent from a neighboring kingdom as a gift. They housed the carousel in the annex, where it was admired and enjoyed during the parties that were held there. The carousel was a gift unlike any other, full of glorious horses, each painted with vibrant colors, their own decorative saddles and glowing hair…all of them, except for one that was different from the rest. Hidden among the rows of horses and other painted creatures, there was one horse that somehow escaped detection. This black, twisted figure almost seemed to be alive, albeit one that was rotting and decaying.

Although the carousel was enjoyed by the court for years, the royal family remained oblivious to the existence of this corpse-like creature.

Lucca remained untouched until word of the plague arrived. The plague ravished the countryside, claiming more lives each day. Like an ominous shadow, it slowly inched towards the unprepared kingdom of Lucca. Out of fear, the royal family and their court abandoned the commoners to save themselves. They believed that once the plague hit, their beloved kingdom would become nothing more than another forgotten place, like all the ancient cities before them. They fled the palace without warning, leaving their people at the mercy of the plague and with no rulers to guide them.

The royal court separated to live in anonymity. Without titles or favor, the former court members settled in the East towards the Adriatic Sea, where they became seafarers. The king, queen, their only son, and the king's father, whose sole title was the King's Consort, fled northwards to Brescia and lived simple, inconspicuous lives. However, it wasn't long before the king and queen contracted the plague they had so desperately tried to escape. Within days, the former rulers of Lucca died in hiding, leaving their only son behind in the care of his grandfather.

Alone in the countryside, the grandfather and the prince lived in a small cottage far away from the rest of civilization, surrounded by nothing but farm animals. The grandfather taught his grandson everything he knew about nature, languages, and art, without ever mentioning his royal claim to the tiny kingdom. However, he did speak of Lucca, mostly through stories which helped put the young prince to sleep as a child. Growing up, the prince never believed that the kingdom of Lucca was actually real. It pained the grandfather to see his grandson living the life of a peasant, especially when he was born for so much more. He wanted to see a crown upon his head, not a pile of hay. His grandfather knew that the young prince needed to return to Lucca, where he could at least be among the people his family had ruled for several generations. But while the grandfather hoped that the plague had not reached his former beloved kingdom, he still feared what might have happened to Lucca if the plague had breached its walls.

It wasn't long before the prince's grandfather passed away, leaving behind the wonderful legacy of Lucca through the stories he told the prince as a child. Before his death, he instructed the prince, who was only seventeen at the time, to leave the countryside. He told his grandson that Lucca did exist and that he must return to the place of his birth, but never to show his face to anyone. Obeying his grandfather, the prince made the journey back to Lucca. Under the cover of darkness, the prince returned and discovered that the small kingdom was untouched by the plague. Surprisingly, Lucca had thrived as a democracy without rulers. The love the people once had for their former rulers appeared to be long forgotten as well. The once regal palace from his grandfather's stories was now covered in dust and overgrown with vines. The prince found the abandoned palace grounds preserved and welcoming, like an elegant sanctuary.

He made his new home within the annexed structure, which was next to the palace. And it was there, in the silence and darkness, that the prince met his first friend, Feletti. He was a young, quick-witted man, who made a living by selling dolls from his private collection. He was well known throughout the kingdom, often drawing crowds when he walked through the streets of Lucca.

However, Feletti was not a true friend to the prince. He had a penchant for creating misery, and even his supposed 'friend' was not excluded from his vicious hobby. Using his natural talents of deception, Feletti told the prince he should hide his face because he was a hideous being who would frighten others. Feletti proclaimed that because he was so hideous, he would surely be rejected by others if he were ever seen.

These words disturbed the young prince, who had looked at his own face several times before. But then he remembered the times his grandfather would stare at him, often in an unsettling way. He also didn't want to disobey his grandfather's orders. In the end, the prince chose to believe Feletti. While exploring alone, he discovered a collection of masks within the palace and annex. The prince decided he would use these to hide his face from view.

He never tired of finding something new, excited to discover that the bedtime stories his grandfather told him were true. However, even when the prince believed he was alone, Feletti was always nearby, in the shadows lurking over him. Over time, the prince became accustomed to Feletti, believing he was the only form of company he truly needed.

However, Feletti's deception went beyond his lies about his friend's appearance. Despite knowing his true identity, he neglected to tell the prince about his royal blood, as well as his own personal history. Devious as he was, Feletti didn't see the harm in keeping a few secrets.

The truth was that Feletti was not a man, and wasn't even human. In fact, he had lived for centuries, and had also known the prince from his birth, having arrived with the prince's first birthday gift, the grand carousel. He had been trapped within that dilapidated horse, which had remained unnoticed among the many rows of other magnificent horses.

When Feletti came out of that decayed shell of a horse, he was nothing more than a weakened, blackened human-like figure with no discernible features. He oozed through the cracks of the wood, sinking and seeping. Feletti eventually found a new form to take which was better suited for his new found freedom. It was sitting upright amongst the others carousel carvings. He was drawn to the permanently painted face and its brightly colored wardrobe, made up of magnificent coats, cloaks and trousers. Taking this new form, Feletti felt alive once more. Breathing again with new life, he decided to put his old talents back to use.

As Feletti's feet clicked and clacked against cobblestone streets, he gazed at a world he had never seen before with sharp eyes. Lucca was bright with smiles and full of promise. It disgusted him. Cracking his fingers and avoiding holy ground, which he was unable to step upon, he studied the people around him. No one seemed to notice his arrival. Feletti would easily be able to begin his life here. He would open a shop that would draw in and change the lives of the people of Lucca.

After promising a shopkeeper the solution to all of his problems in exchange for his business, Feletti established his shop, 'Dream Dolls'. His shop did not run like any of the other businesses in town. He dealt in dreams and barters of high consequence instead of money. Despite this, customers never stopped coming through his door and Feletti never had any reason to leave Lucca. Even though the people of Lucca prospered, it was never enough for them. The kingdom was always full of desperate people who wanted to know if wishes could come true.

One day, a curious and timid customer came to Feletti's shop, seeking his aid. Feletti had seen this man press his face against the glass multiple times, looking like a starving child, before finally entering the shop. The man had recently lost his wife. His son was his only reason to continue living. He came to Feletti on his knees, eyes wet, begging him for the daughter his wife had always wanted. The perfect daughter, who would make all men falter at the sight of her. Someone who could cook the most delicious meals in the world. Someone pure. Intrigued by the request, Feletti decided to give this man one of his most coveted and beloved dolls. She was young, with eyes deeper than the night sky full of stars. Her hair was as soft as the silk her dress was made of. Her skin was untouched, like her small hands, which had never carried a single tool, other than a spoon. Her face seemed to radiate eternal innocence and beauty.

Feletti transformed the doll into a young girl. Letting out a gasp and embracing the girl, the man declared her to be perfect. But before she was given to him, Feletti asked for one condition. Upon his time and choosing, the girl would become a doll again and rejoin his collection. The man agreed, already overwhelmed with the joy of having his own daughter. The former doll showed no outward signs of her former self. Her skin was flushed a healthy pink. Her hands were warm. When she flexed her fingers, her movements were as graceful as a bird. She was no longer on display in the shop window. She was alive.

The man raised her as his own, remembering his wife every time he marveled at the girl's flawless features. Her striking blue eyes sparkled against her dark brown hair, which bounced with her every effortless movement. He practically strutted about the streets, always keeping her by his side. Every man and woman in the kingdom admired and envied the man's family that was now complete with his new daughter. Until the day he finally joined his wife, the girl brought him eternal happiness.

Chapter One

St. Anselm's Day

Everything was black. Silent. Peaceful and quiet, until music began to play. The tune started off slow, the notes played gently upon polished keys. The keys responded to the tender touch of firm fingertips. Soon the tune turned into an eerie song, which rang out clearly and distinctly in the darkness.

The song started low, full of rich detail and desire. This quiet tune grew louder, slowly inching towards her. But she was fast asleep, and the music didn't wake her. She was lying on the ground, wearing a glamorous gown with long sleeves that puffed near her shoulders. The dress flowed from her waist to her feet, like a rose in bloom. She slept peacefully, cradling her head on top of her arm, while stretching out the other. She was content, unaware of the approaching music. As he continued to play the song, he smiled faintly as she began to hear the notes.

The room began to sway, like flower-covered swings in the wind. The music began to torment her. She winced and frowned as though she were struggling. He moved closer to her, wearing an unsettling and nightmarish grin, and found her asleep on the floor. Although she was sleeping, she was awake in her own dreamland. The music grew even louder. The room swayed forcefully, until...

"Marian!"

Marian shook her head, realizing she was standing in the middle of the street. She was completely surrounded by large crowds of people, who were cheering and celebrating St. Anselm's Day. Her older brother, Placido, called her name above the crowd of people. He cupped his hands around his mouth and shouted,

"Marian! You're going to miss the horses."

Marian's eyes barely shifted from the slightly damaged accordion, which was sitting behind the glass window of the shop in front of her. All of the keys remained untouched. However, the shredding straps and bellows showed signs of abuse. The price tag, which was now covered in dust, had been changed several times but never attracted a buyer. Turning away and looking past her brother, Marian saw the grand horses arrive. They were decorated with brightly colored saddles, pulling along their wagons. Children sat on the back of the wagons, tossing flowers and small pieces of candy to the eager crowds. The smell of cooked veal with rice from the stationed wagons and carts, which had been brought all the way from the Arab world, filled her nostrils.

The beautiful sight distracted Marian instantly. She smiled and tried to catch the flower petals floating weightless in the air. She leapt, catching some of the petals in her hand and caressing them with her fingertips. A few young men watched her from across the street, whistling and tipping their hats upon seeing Marian's nimble and graceful leaps. They wore tightly fitted pants, shiny boots, and breeches, with tiny brim hats which barely covered their thick and wavy hair. The young men disguised their gawking by lowering their heads, hiding their stares underneath their hats. Her radiance had captivated them. As it often did.

"Marian! Don't wander off!" Placido called out to his sister with more force, cupping his hands around his mouth again.

Marian stopped jumping, satisfied with the amount of petals she had captured. She opened the threaded and beaded pouch hanging from her waist and placed the petals inside. A few children almost tripped over her feet as they rushed past, trying to catch the petals which were falling like snow.

Frustrated, Placido pushed through the crowd and moved towards Marian. He pushed the longer strands of his light blond hair behind his ears in order to see better, and nearly tripped over his worn boots trying to reach his sister again.

Upon fixing the bottom of her dress Marian glanced upward and spotted Placido looking upon her as he did many times before. She had no excuse and simply followed next to him as he moved away from the large crowd.

T ogether they wandered to a nearby table, which stretched the length of several storefronts. They grabbed plates full of rice and moved towards the delicious lasagna and fresh bottles of wine. Placido picked up a goblet full of wine, leaning over without disrupting the couple next to him. Holding the goblet in his left hand, he lifted it up and inhaled the scent of the wine. He swirled the nectar inside the goblet, watching the red stream dance in circles. The smell brought back memories of his father.

"May I try some?" Marian asked, watching her brother play with the wine. He smiled.

"I'm not sure. I thought you didn't like wine," he said raising a brow.

Marian frowned. "That was last time and you tricked me. Please?"

"Just one sip." He handed her the wine from his rugged hand. Eagerly, Marian took a large gulp but nearly spit it out when she tried to swallow. The taste was overpowering and her delicate frame couldn't handle it once again. Placido took the wine from her and laughed, wondering how a beautiful girl could have such childish mannerisms.

When Marian caught her breath she looked to Placido with a silent warning before a loud voice caught their attention.

"Placido! Placido!"

A mustached man, who was cooking veal over a fire, called him over. His long vest covered most of his body, almost reaching his knees.

Placido and Marian walked towards him, passing by a large

orchestra which was getting ready to perform for a small crowd of families patiently waiting. The siblings were greeted with hugs and kisses on the cheek.

"Both of you have grown so much! And Marian, look at you! Still so young and beautiful. A masterpiece!" He laughed joyously.

"Grazie Roberto." She thanked with a small curtsy.

"Placido, you better be careful. Soon you'll be discussing wedding plans and meeting her suitor. Perhaps one of my sons, Marian?"

Marian's voice suddenly disappeared. Her mind went blank at the thought of marriage. The idea of her life changing permanently was something she hadn't quite grasped. Clearing her throat, she tried to speak up but struggled to find the words as images of herself in a gown before a large crowded cathedral made her slightly tremble.

"Oh…I haven't-"

"When she perfects certain meals, perhaps then she'll be able to meet your sons," Placido interrupted.

Marian glanced at her brother and he winked to her with reassurance.

"Yes, very true. Although they are eager to see you. So, when is your toy shop going to open? My little ones keep asking me to buy toys. But I keep telling them I can't because the store is closed. And everyone knows buying toys from another town is expensive," Roberto complained, handing over plates of veal to two young men.

Placido nodded, before wincing at the loud sizzle of the water boiling over the open fire.

"It will be open soon. Marian just finished the detailing around the windows. She's working on the table cloths now," he explained and turned to smile at his sister.

Marian had several talents outside of cooking that she was

proud of. It meant so much to her that Placido was equally proud.

"I look forward to seeing the final touches. The table cloth you stitched for us last Christmas is beautiful. My wife adores it!" Roberto winked and Marian blushed.

"Grazie," she replied quietly, afraid to make eye contact after the awkward discussion of marriage.

"Placido, is it too early to place a request for my children?"

"Not at all. In fact…"

Marian stopped listening to Placido's conversation as the eerie sound of an accordion began to play nearby. Her delicate ears recognized the notes, and it seemed like the music was coming closer. Marian roughly bit down on her lip. She started looking around frantically, trying to find the source of the music.

As she looked away, she saw a group of children stop dead in their tracks and suddenly change direction, following the music as though they were being called towards it. Marian searched for the source of the horrible song, her stomach tying itself into painful knots as the music grew louder and louder. She tried to cover her ears, praying for the music to stop, when she suddenly heard his name.

"Feletti!"

A few mothers pulled their children back, holding them close to their sides. Others allowed their children to rush towards the well-dressed and popular man. He wore a fitted jacket, high boots that were tucked into tightly fitted pants, and a stitched hat that had several feathers tied together with a thick, dark red sash made of satin. Marian saw him stop behind several groups of people talking over each other, only several feet away from her. Although they were loud, the music overpowered their voices. Feletti transitioned to his mandolin, continuing to play his song, now surrounded by a circle of children. He moved his legs up and down to the beat of the song.

After the song was finished, he revealed a stack of sugar canes from his pocket.

"Come children. Come and enjoy the finest of foreign delicacies," Feletti called out, holding the sugar canes in his hands.

The children rushed forward, each receiving a pat on the head. They laughed and took the candy, eating it like rabbits until their hearts sang with delight. Out of the corner of his eye, Feletti noticed one boy in particular. He was staying as far away from the other children as possible. The boy was barely four years old and wore a dark green carpenter's cap that almost covered his entire head. The familiarity surrounding the young boy was like a dense fog. After a moment of deep thought, Feletti remembered.

"Little Luigi, I remember you. You don't like sugar canes do you?" he asked.

The little boy shook his head, covering his mouth with his hands. Feletti grinned at his rather shy response.

"That's right. I think I may have something else you like." He reached into one of the seven pockets in his long coat. "Ah hah. For you." He pulled out a large date, handing it over to the child with his thin fingers. Luigi smiled and took the date while his parents kept a close eye watching Feletti's every move.

"That's my doll. Stay away from sugar," he said, fixing the cap on the boy's head.

Luigi skipped back to his parents, who were waiting for him away from the crowd of children.

Marian watched, unable to look away. Sweat began to form over her brow, tickling her skin. She had always been terrified of Feletti for reasons she never understood, and she didn't have the nerve to find out why.

Later that night, Placido worked on some shelves for the shop, while Marian prepared dinner in the small kitchen a few rooms away. She had already finished baking the bread and a fruit pie for dessert. The pasta was almost done, already filling the room with a warm scent. She added a few extra ingredients into the sauce and lightly stirred. Marian always felt peaceful when she cooked and baked. It was one of her only pleasures in life.

With an exhausted sigh, Placido came into the kitchen. He was looking for an old cloth to bandage the small cut on his hand. Smelling the sauce, he looked over to the pot, only to have Marian shoo him away with a wave of her hand.

"It's almost done," Marian said, continuing to stir the sauce methodically.

"I can't wait any longer! Your cooking is the best in all of Lucca. The Pope is unfortunate that he doesn't eat food like this," Placido exclaimed. He took a piece of cloth out of a nearby drawer to tend to his wound.

Marian tasted the sauce before replying. "I think the Pope eats very well. Personally, I look forward to the pie more than the pasta."

"Yes, you do love your sweets. Just like a child willing to spoil their dinner." Placido nodded, wrapping the cloth tightly around his hand. He bit on his lip, feeling the burn of his open wound across his hand.

Marian glanced over at Placido and noticed the red tint in the cloth, which was slowly seeping through the threaded fabric like a wave. She stared at the red stain, that strange hue which she never saw on her own skin. Marian turned her right hand over, looking at her palm. Her skin was smooth and untouched, as she had always remembered it to be. Never pricked, not even by a needle.

Out of the corner of her eye, Marian watched as Placido wrapped the cloth completely around his hand, applying pressure to the wound. As he stood up, she turned back to the pot, tasting the sauce one last time before serving dinner.

Chapter Two

The Giant Key

"Come, come! Auction at the royal palace today! All are welcome!"

Placido and Marian headed towards the abandoned palace, moving alongside the growing crowd of interested buyers. Placido looked around, surprised at the number of people who were coming. The grand auction was set-up right outside the locked gates that barred the only access to the palace grounds. Marian stared past the gates and at the palace, which looked as though it was miles away. The royal playground was eerily silent and empty. In the distance, she could see that the gardens had decayed. The remaining plant life did not compare to the grand flowers which used to blossom, fed by the statues that no longer flowed with water. It was a ghost of what it once was.

No one had entered the palace since it was abandoned, left to rot in the aftermath of a plague that never came to Lucca. A tragic miscalculation that led to a great betrayal. This was why the royal auction was being held, to finally put an end to the lingering memory of the king and queen, the rulers who abandoned their people. How could they have done so without remorse or regret? To flee without warning and leave their people who adored them to a horrific fate.

"Gather round everyone! Gather round, the auction is about to begin! Hurry! Hurry!"

The crowd gathered around the auction stand, looking at the display which contained almost a hundred items from the palace. All of these priceless pieces were undamaged, artifacts that hadn't been handled or seen for years. Everyone's eyes glowed at the prospects of what each item could bring them.

These were priceless items that if it weren't for the king and queen's departure, none would be able to even look upon them! Such a lavish lifestyle was hidden from them for so long.

"Feel free to look as long as you like everyone! There will be plenty of items for sale and auction! Take your time! No need to push!"

Placido pulled Marian along, squeezing her hand tightly as the crowd moved closer. He moved towards the display with determination as everyone around him voiced what items they already wanted. Finding a good spot to examine the palace artifacts, he began to look for anything that piqued his interest. Over half of the auctioned items were gifts the people of Lucca had given the royal family, and they were eager to get them back. Many couples observed the queen's jewelry collection, admiring the antique necklaces, rings, and earrings made of gold and silver. The gems and jewels shined brightly in the sunlight, casting a rainbow of colors upon the ground. As gorgeous as those items were and how unique they would be, Marian had no interest.

Instead she wandered off to the side where she found a display with hand sewn dolls. They were dressed in long gowns and masquerade masks, and placed in a tower for exhibition. Marian trailed her fingers down the table cloths, which were embroidered with familiar patterns of the royal seal. The teal embroidery gleamed in the sunlight, standing out against the other items that seemed to blend together. But the dolls intrigued her. Each doll had a different design, each of them clearly made with their own personality. As she handled the dolls, Marian realized she knew their names, place of origin, and destined futures.

She frowned, glancing at them. She recognized their design

and posture and tried to understand where she had seen them before. She could hear the large sounds of the crowd slowly fade as she focused on the dolls that appeared to be looking at her.

"Marian!" Placido called.

She looked up, noticing that her brother was calling her over. She was barely able to see him amongst the men who were purchasing gifts for their wives and fiancés. Marian left the doll display feeling slightly confused and returned to his side. Next to them, a married couple purchased a small night stand with intricate carvings that looked like it took years to craft. They paid the auctioneer in full, hoping to claim a set of candelabras next. Placido watched as the striking young woman praised her love, placing one hand on his back and the other on his chest. She gave him a kiss as he hauled the night stand onto a cart with ease. The rest of the crowd continued to examine the items on display, including sets of furniture, dining ware, and clothing.

Placido focused his attention back to the item he desired to buy.

"I think I found something we could use," he said with certainty.

Placido was looking at a large object which was resting against a dining table, nearly hidden among the rest of the furniture in the display.

"Marian, what do you think of that?" he asked, pointing straight ahead.

"What is it?" Marian stared at the large object. It was something she had never seen before.

He shook his head baffled, stroking his chin with his fingers. The object was rounded on what appeared to be the top, skinny in the middle, and with the bottom shaped like an odd square.

"I'm not sure. Maybe…a key? A wooden…key?" Placido guessed.

"What would you use it for?" Marian questioned.

Placido tried to explain even to himself why he would need such an oddly shaped object. It was obvious why no one else wanted it.

"It would make an interesting door inside the shop! I need to separate the shop and my workshop in the back. I've been avoiding buying a door but…I need this," he explained, staring at the item as though he were studying some kind of wild animal.

He held out his hands to measure the width of the key, hoping no one else would notice. Placido could picture the perfect space in his shop for the key. It would fit easily in the space and bring a whole new kind of attention to his shop. He had to make efforts to separate himself from future competitors.

"Nice eye, Placido! Are you interested in the key?" the auctioneer asked, stepping towards the siblings with a loud voice.

Marian looked at him silently as another couple kissed each other lovingly while two men carried what looked like a bed frame for them.

"I am. I think it will work," Placido replied confidently.

"Very well. Have you seen anything you want Marian?" he asked her hoping she would say yes.

She glanced over to the table which held the collection of dolls, debating grabbing at least one doll. While she knew she would cherish it, she felt guilty for desiring something her brother would call, "childish".

"No. Thank you," she lied, returning her attention to the wooden key and folding her hands in front of her.

"Very well! Placido buys the giant wooden key! Placido! Buys the wooden key!" the auctioneer bellowed to the crowd.

As the auctioneer waved some young men over to move the other pieces of furniture away from it, Marian stared at the giant key. After the auctioneer took off the red tag and started cleaning the key, she tilted her head to the side to get a better look at it. Marian still found the giant key to be extremely puzzling.

'What purpose would a giant key serve?' she wondered.

Hours later, the large key was bolted gently to the door frame inside the toy shop. Marian watched Placido as he struggled to hold the key upright in the glow of the lit candles that surrounded the room. By now, the sun was almost gone as the darkened night sky began to appear. She tilted her head, continuing to stare at the key. She tried to understand the purpose of this giant key, and how it would function as a door. But if there was anything she knew about her brother, it was that he was creative and able to make things that many would never be able to conceive. Placido grunted, while sweat rolled down the side of his face. His struggle finally ended when he heard a small 'click.' Once the key was locked into the doorframe, he pushed the key back and forth, watching it open and close with ease. Thankfully, the wooden beams provided enough support for the key to hold. Money well spent in his opinion.

"Perfecto!" he announced, proud but slightly out of breath. Placido beamed as he examined the new addition to the shop, before wiping the sweat off his forehead.

"What do you think sister?" he asked, turning to face her with an exuberant expression.

"Well…it's different," she replied with uncertainty with her head still tilted.

"Marian, don't do that to your neck. Look at it now," he said with a sigh. Placido moved Marian's head back to its upright position.

"It's…different." Marian sighed, while her brother grinned and lifted up his hands. He was clearly proud of the achievement.

"Exactly. Different in a way that will separate me from my future competitors. I think we can open shop by the end of the week. We'll have a grand opening! The newest toy shop to open in Lucca!"

Chapter Three

Rain From Heaven

Marian thanked the baker, placing the giant loaf of semolina bread underneath the cloth inside her basket. As she paid him, the bright sun was suddenly swallowed by thick grey clouds. She looked up, smelling the scent of rain in the air.

"It looks like rain is coming. Better get home quickly Marian," the baker warned, observing the changing sky.

Marian nodded in agreement. "I will. Grazie."

Marian alternated from a light jog to a sprint, until the first few raindrops fell from the sky. Within seconds, heavy rain started falling. She was too late. Marian felt the tiny drops of rain washing over her face, which increased at an alarming speed when a swift wind picked up from seemingly nowhere. The droplets struck her fair skin and braided hair.

She wrapped her shawl over her head tightly, looking for the nearest source of shelter alongside other people in the street, all of whom were running for cover. One shop after another closed their doors and windows as the rain poured down. The water filled small gutters, open barrels, and buckets, and quickly overflowed from the containers onto the soft, spongy ground. Marian ran, splashing through puddles, until she found the annexed structure next to the abandoned palace.

The building was separated from the palace, being outside of its walls. It was hidden behind several abandoned wagons, rundown vehicles which had yet to be moved. While she was slightly afraid to enter such a place, she didn't see another option. Picking up the bottom of her soaking dress, Marian pulled the broken wooden wheels aside from her path, while also moving aside pieces of splintered wood and broken plaster vases. Exhausted, Marian made her way to the annexed structure's entrance and pushed against the heavy doors. She peered inside the silent building almost afraid of what she would find. Although the damp air and dead silence were unnerving, Marian couldn't help but walk inside. This place was a new discovery, and she wasn't going to pass up this opportunity to explore.

The floor was pure marble, brightened by the glass domed ceiling, which had minor cracks etched into the metal frames. Marian could see her reflection in the marble floor as she took cautious steps. The walls were draped in dozens of long white linen sheets. While some statues were silhouetted underneath these sheets, others were only partially draped, exposing interesting shapes and poses.

Marian removed her shawl, astounded by the size of the room. Her wet shoes slapped against the floor creating a light echo. Marian barely managed to grasp onto the basket, almost letting it slip out of her hands several times distracted by such whimsical majesty. As she walked across the room, she listened to the rain bouncing off the large structure. Her steps became slower. She passed by the statues, sometimes touching the hands that were extended, as though they wanted to be held. Marian was barely able to see that, behind the statues, there were several mirrors covered in sheets. The frames of the mirrors were engraved, with some cracked in half. She walked forward, listening to the peaceful silence of the room, when she noticed for the first time that the floor was clean. Marian found it a little odd that an abandoned building had been cleaned so recently. She didn't linger on the thought, however, when she discovered a strange carousel in her midst. While she approached the carousel, a small smile formed on her face and her eyes widened with delight.

Marian had heard about this exclusive form of entertainment for the royal family and court in stories, but had never seen it for herself. The giant carousel, half covered in fallen sheets from the walls, remained in the shadows as if on purpose. She could smell the carousel's fading, pleasing aroma of flowers and age. The ride was a towering monument. The top looked like a Cirque tent, but was shaped like a bloomed flower. Underneath the coating of dust and spider webs, Marian could see the silver and blue paint of the carousel. Taking small steps around the carousel, she noticed each horse was unique and different, although they were all equally magnificent. The horses appeared to be painted with every color known throughout the world. Every horse was designed with perfect detail, from the tassels on their saddles and even to the curls in their wild hair. From every tooth, leg, and scuff on their hooves, the horses were vividly depicted. They almost seemed alive.

Walking around the carousel, she imagined the charming, childlike music it must have played before. None of the horses showed any sign of damage. They were sitting, waiting to be enjoyed again by the very people who abandoned it. Looking down, she noticed each hoof was made of gold. The rotating poles that held the horses were also golden. Even their eye lashes were painted with gold foil.

As Marian circled the magnificent carousel, which was far bigger than she expected, she noticed a strange device. She came to a halt, staring at the object. It was almost completely covered by an old rug and tapestry. The device was blue and shaped like a square, covered in dust and cobwebs. Marian stared at the blue device, noticing a large gap in the center. She placed her hand inside and felt around, tracing her fingers around the oddly shaped device. Her fingers danced around the edges, until she saw her reflection in one of the carousel mirrors. In the foreground of her reflection, she noticed one horse in particular. This horse was different from the others.

Stepping onto the wooden platform, she locked her fingers around a horse's saddle for support. As Marian passed the other horses, she began to feel sick. Her stomach started to churn the deeper she moved within the carousel itself. Her curiosity was burning inside of her like a growing flame. Despite her uneasiness, Marian found herself being drawn towards this one horse all the way in the back. Passing several rows of horses and seats, she stopped right before reaching the horse, suddenly afraid to take another step forward. The horse was painted black. An odd, thick, slimly substance covered its hooves and hair. It was skinnier than the other horses, having a sickly and decaying appearance. The horse had tangled hair, cracked and sharpened teeth, red and dark brown eyes, with drool coming from its mouth. She noticed there was a very long and deep crack running through the saddle.

Deeply unsettled, Marian stepped away from this disturbing creature, when she realized she couldn't hear the rain anymore. She ran off of the carousel to look up at the glass ceiling. The clouds were suddenly parting. The rain, which had started off as a violent downpour, had slowed down. Now there were only gentle raindrops tapping the glass ceiling. The local cathedral bell rang out several times, startling her.

"Is that…is that the time already?" she asked herself aloud. Marian tucked the bread deeper into her basket, while also tugging her shawl back over her hair and face.

"I have to get home. I have to get home. I have to get home. Have to make dinner. Have to make dinner." She repeated this mantra to herself, ashamed of having been so easily distracted. Marian quickly moved towards the exit, leaving as fast as she could without once glancing back at the world the royal family had left behind.

During dinner, Marian's thoughts were occupied with the oddly shaped blue box, more so than the disturbing black horse. She watched Placido enjoy his meal, constantly smiling and nodding with every bite. Aside from his constant noises of enjoyment, the room was silent. Marian kept debating when to speak up. She kept her legs crossed at her ankles, rocking back and forth, while also trying to eat the meal she had made.

"Brother?" she eventually asked.

"Yes?" he replied, taking another fork full of pasta.

She hesitated, folding her delicate hands in her lap debating if she should even ask him. Leaning forward, she finally asked, "The structure next to the royal palace…outside the wall? What is it?"

Placido looked up at the ceiling, pondering while he answered. "The annexed building? I believe that was…where the parties were held," he said.

"Did you ever attend one, before I was born?"

"No. Only the royal family and their court were allowed to attend. People like us would have never been invited." Placido looked down at his plate before continuing.

"Speaking of, the Friuli's purchased the entire dining set from the auction yesterday."

"They did?"

"Yes. The actual dining table of the royal family. All one hundred and twenty pieces for their daughter and her soon-to-be husband." He paused, observing Marian's expression upon hearing the last part before continuing. "They deserve something luxurious, if not more."

He took another bite of his food before speaking again. "Their youngest son however wants a puppy in the worst way. With his birthday coming soon, they want to give him one, but I doubt they'll be able to afford it now. Nearly every last cent they had is for the wedding."

Marian nodded, eyeing the pie she had baked on the table not far from them. The top was decorated with light sugar and she had added sprinkled candies around the crooked edges. Her mouth watered, dying to eat a slice of it before she finished dinner. She wanted to taste something sweet.

"Not until after you finish dinner," Placido reminded her with a firm nod.

Marian pouted, staring at the alluring pie full of deep pomegranate juice and sugar.

"I'm not a child Placido. I can eat sweets before dinner if I want," she replied, a little annoyed.

"But you are younger than me. And it's my responsibility to take care of you."

"Because father and mother aren't here."

Placido hesitated before responding, staring deeply into her doe like eyes. He noticed a shimmer to them he couldn't quite recall ever seeing before. After a brief flash of his father's distressed expression crossed his mind, he finally spoke. "Because I want to. You're my sister, until the end. I want what's best for you."

"Which means me getting married right? Is that what's best for me?"

"Marian-"

"You don't have to…say it." Marian's eyes nearly glowed as she tried to find her voice and a way to explain her frustration.

"I know that is what you want for me. That is what father and mother would want for me."

"It's your duty Marian. You cannot live here with me forever no matter how much you want to."

"Can't I?" she asked with almost pleading eyes.

"Marian, if you're worried about finding a husband or finding one who will take care of you-"

"I'm worried about everything changing."

Placido took in her words hearing a hint of sadness in her tone. She looked as though she was going to cry at any moment. Seeing her cry for even the smallest of reasons broke him.

"Just because you will marry does not mean I would stop existing. I will be here for you. I will always be here and love you. Yes, you will not be living here anymore. Yes, you will have a husband who will take care of you. But that doesn't mean you and I become strangers." He paused, trying to gauge Marian's reaction.

"Let's not talk about this anymore tonight. Let us enjoy our dinner and dessert. Alright?"

"Yes." Marian responded lowly. "Placido, I love you too."

After dinner and dessert, Marian watched Placido put the finishing touches on the outside of the toy shop. She wrapped the shawl around her shoulders, glancing at the night sky, which was lit up by the moon and stars. The rain clouds had long since passed on, but the remnants of the storm were still in every small puddle and full barrel. Next door, she could hear their neighbors finishing their dinner. The sound of utensils and messy plates being gathered muffled their voices. Turning her attention back to the shop, she noticed the calming glow of the candelabra in the front window. Above the door, "Placido's Toys" shined in painted letters.

Placido stepped down from the wooden ladder before admiring his finished work. He smiled, deeply satisfied with his accomplishment. He was ready to begin his new future, making toys for children and for those who were older but young at heart.

"Father would be very proud of you," Marian said.

"He is. I know he's here with us. Mother too," Placido replied.

Marian glanced inside the shop, looking at the detailed border she had painted around the sides and corners of the bay window. She indeed did beautiful work as Placido was told numerous times that evening alone by passers by. Some children had already begun peeking through the window, anxious for when they will receive a new toy to play with. As Marian looked further inside the toy shop, she could see the finished shelves placed perfectly and neatly. The room was glowing in the candlelight and of course the giant key against the door frame was noticeably standing in its proper place. Her eyes widened when she noticed the odd design the teeth were shaped into. She tilted her head downward and walked forward, holding out her hands.

"Marian? What are you doing?" Placido chuckled at her

strange and sudden movement.

"Nothing. I thought…I saw something," she said, walking back to the shop. Placido followed her inside, shaking his head.

"You shouldn't do that, you'll hurt yourself. It's high time you go to bed. Tomorrow will be a busy day and we'll both be needing the rest."

Marian nodded in response as she approached the key. Her eyes remained focused on its odd shape. She touched the indents and pattern of the teeth. The discovery suddenly clicked in her mind, like clockwork.

'This IS a key after all!'

Chapter Four

The Many Masks of Man

The next day, Marian could hardly contain herself after the discovery she had made. She waited until her brother left the shop with a majority of his toys. He was going to perform his first demonstration of the handmade toys before a promising crowd. Before he left, Placido reminded her that the grand opening of the shop would take place that evening which meant almost everything was riding on his demonstration. This would be a grand opening for the kingdom, and the beginning of his new future in toy making. He put love into all of his creations, designing every toy, placing each of them into a soft bag and wrapping them in satin.

Marian observed the way he handled each toy with such a delicate nature. For as long as she could remember, this was his dream and he wouldn't let anyone convince him to pursue other passions. Once Placido began speaking to the large crowd of children and their families, Marian dashed back to the shop as fast as she could. Inside the shop, Marian struggled but eventually managed to pry the giant key from its bolts off the doorway. For a brief moment she hesitated, wondering how Placido would react to it's disappearance. She refused to dwell on those thoughts. Lifting it up the first time, she nearly dropped the key onto her small feet, ripping the bottom of her full length dress. She sighed, seeing the tear across her dark purple dress. It would cost a small fortune to fix.

As she tried to lift the key again, the weight of it surprised her. Marian had expected the key to be an immovable force, impossible to drag; but once she moved it onto a wheelbarrow it became a little easier.

Marian struggled at first pushing the wheelbarrow through the streets, making her way to the mysterious annexed building. She hesitated before opening the large doors, feeling weak from having pushed the key across town. Lugging the key from the wheelbarrow, she winced every time the key screeched and scraped against the marble floor. Marian watched her own reflection in the floor as she approached the carousel, relieved that her task was almost complete. Thanks to the glowing sun, the room was now brightly lit. Tossing the carpet and tapestry aside from the blue box, she struggled but eventually lifted the key towards the lock.

'This is a lock and this is the key to open it! It has to be! What other key could possibly be big enough to fit inside?' she thought to herself with confidence.

Dropping the key into the lock, she heard a snap. The key was now tightly fastened inside. She smiled at her accomplishment, breathing heavily as her lungs begged for rest. Exhausted, Marian rolled up her sleeves and tied them with the ribbons from her dress. She braced herself for the more difficult part.

Marian pushed herself onto the wooden key, wrapping her arms around and turning it until she heard a strange sound. A gentle but eerie tune began to play from seemingly everywhere at once. The louder it grew, the more pleasing it became. The carousel lights turned on with a hum, and the room was suddenly filled with glowing light. As the carousel began to spin, the horses started moving, up and down in a soothing motion. She watched it spin, tugging the sheets and dusty webs away. Marian watched her reflection in the mirrors pass by several times as an overwhelming sense of joy filled her body. She trotted alongside the moving horses with her outstretched arms feeling as though she was flying.

Feeling brave, she leaped onto the wooden platform. Holding onto one of the horses, she examined her reflection more closely in the mirrors that adorned the center of the carousel. She placed her hands across the center of the machine, wiping away years of dust and discovering lush hues of blues, greens, yellows, and pinks. As the carousel continued to spin, she breathed deeply and exhaled. Her happiness grew and blossomed while she watched the gentle movements of the horses and the revolving carousel. Marian had never felt such joy in her life.

She wrapped her hands around the nearest golden pole holding one of the horses. Resting her face against the cool metal, she felt stray strands of her thick, brown hair brush past her eyes and tickle her nose. Turning her head, Marian looked behind her observing the elegant flow of each horse moving in rhythm. Her eyes spotted seats on the carousel, attached to the hard floor. They were shaped into swans and other creatures with magnificent wings and expressive gestures. She walked towards them carefully, holding onto a horse with each step, when she saw a black blanket covering one of the seats. Curious, she carefully pulled off the blanket. Marian discovered a young man who was lying down, fast asleep. His long legs were bent inward and both of his hands were clasped shut, resting under his head like a pillow.

"Who is this?" she asked aloud, completely bewildered and stunned at the sight.

The young man seemed to be older than herself, dressed in dark blue and black clothing with tints of gold. His soft hair draped onto the detailed ceramic mask which covered his entire face. Marian sat down on the seat as slowly as she could, while staring at the bright green and white detailed mask. He didn't move or stir at her presence. As she lowered her hands to touch the mask, Marian watched his chest rise and fall with each breath. Feeling the roughly painted texture with her fingers, she traced the features of the mask imagining the kind of person whom could create such artwork with mere paintbrushes. Gently, she tried to remove the mask without disturbing him. The mask slid off his face, brushing his hair forward in a swift movement. Upon seeing the man's face, she let out a gasp, nearly dropping the mask onto the floor.

He opened his eyes, revealing a light shade of brown color, much like tree bark. Immediately, he noticed that his mask was missing. He looked up to see a strange girl who was looking over him, wearing a terrified, yet awestruck, expression.

"My mask!" he shouted in a panic. The young man covered his face with both hands, shaking violently.

"You're…you're-"

"Please don't look at me. Don't look at me! Please….go," he said quickly. The young man leapt from the seat like a startled cat, his hands still covering his face. He jumped off the carousel with ease and moved into the shadows.

"Wait, I'm sorry if I scared you!" Marian called. She tried to follow him, but nearly tripped over her own feet.

He turned a corner and disappeared from her sight like a shadow in the night. Running to the key, Marian pushed herself against it, trying to turn the carousel off. She grunted, forcing all of her weight onto the key, but to no avail. Confused, she tried again, before noticing that she was being tugged backwards. Marian turned around and saw that the back of her dress, which had a long, crisscrossed ribbon tied around her waist, was caught in between the wooden platform of the carousel and the lock.

In a fright Marian let out a cry, trying to free herself. The back of her dress ripped loudly, sending a cold sensation through her frame. She tugged at the material in a panic before the mysterious young man came out of the shadows. He pushed the key to a halt, using his legs and his feet as the carousel slowed to a stop. As the horses slowed down, the music and lights faded away filling the room with an even more eerie silence than the first time she entered.

Marian didn't speak. She could feel the rip in the back of her dress, which trailed all the way up to her waist. She felt embarrassed, heartbroken and frozen on the spot. Marian stared at the tattered ends of her ribbon and the pieces of her dress on the floor. Her heart wouldn't stop racing. She tugged at the ripped ends of her dress, trying to hold it together, when she noticed the young man slowly removing himself from the carousel. He didn't speak either. They stared at each other like two different species of animals meeting for the first time. Taking deep breaths, he practically stomped towards her at an alarming pace. Marian backed into one of the horses, unable to move any further. She was intimidated by his sudden, advancing steps.

No word slipped out from his lips. Not that any words needed to. His eyes told her everything she needed to know. Marian could see her reflection in his striking eyes. Suddenly, he retrieved his mask from where she had dropped it and quickly put it back onto his face. He stared into her eyes through the open holes of his mask.

"Please. I'm sorry," Marian said, while keeping herself against the horse.

"How did you find the key?" he asked in response. His voice was as clear as the sky after a terrible storm.

Unable to answer immediately, her eyes wandered to the pattern on his clothing. Marian recognized the familiar royal hues of teal and black, the unmistakable crown and angelic faces which were sewn onto the cloth. She frowned. "I purchased it," Marian finally replied. "It was during the palace auction."

He turned to the carousel, staring at himself in one of the mirrors, several rows behind where Marian stood. Looking away from his reflection, he asked, "And you knew how to bring the carousel back to life?"

"Lucky guess? I'm sorry." She couldn't help looking back at him, back into his eyes that somehow lured her in.

"Don't look at me. I'm a monster," he growled. His voice echoed inside the room and Marian shook at his tone.

But in spite of herself, she leaned forward. She loosened her grip on the horse, while still trying to contain the back of her dress. "Is that why you wear a mask?" she asked.

"Yes!" he shouted. "I freed you. Now go!" He pointed towards the entrance of the annexed building.

"Sir, you are not a monster."

"You lie!"

"If you were a monster, you would have never saved me,"

Marian argued.

He lowered his arm and stared at her. Unnerved by the intensity of his eyes, she watched uneasily as he hunched over, as though he was getting ready to attack.

"What did you just say?" he whispered.

"I saw your face. You aren't a monster. You are…handsome."

The young man shook his head. He let out a chuckle of disbelief. "Please. Just leave." He moved to the side, allowing her to pass.

Marian moved away from the carousel, carefully stepping around the masked young man. She was still suspicious, worried even that he was going to harm her. But even as Marian started walking back towards the entrance, she couldn't help gazing back at him over her shoulder. He lowered his head and let out a deep sigh. Marian started to speak again, when she heard him say,

"I don't know why I saved you. Just go. Don't come back, and don't look for me. Ever."

Chapter Five

My Name is Princio

The next morning, news spread fast about the successful grand opening of the toy shop the night before. Placido received a warm congratulations as each customer swarmed his toy shop while Marian refrained from being present. She occasionally spoke to customers out of mere politeness, but her mind was far from the joyous moment for her brother. Instead she worried about her brother's reaction to the missing key. Throughout the evening toys were sold and orders were placed at a fast pace. Several times, Marian tried to tell Placido what had happened in the annexed building. As much as she feared his anger, she needed to tell him. He needed to know. She even brought out the ripped gown, which she loved so much. But every time she tried to speak with her brother, he was unable to answer, preoccupied with the shop and its many customers. Eventually, she gave up. Talking about what happened wouldn't make any difference. Instead, Marian decided to busy herself with preparations for the Dessert Pie contest, something she looked forward to every year.

That very morning she had baked something she knew was going to please the crowd. She had done this many times before and by now her baking skills were near instinct.

"And today's winner for most delicious pie goes to…Marian!"

The crowd rejoiced, throwing flower petals into the air while her competitors applauded her grandly. Marian smiled brightly, leaping forward to claim her prize with much eagerness. A flower crown was placed upon her head, before she was awarded with a delicate necklace made of gold.

Within the crowd, Placido whistled loudly, applauding his sister. If toy making was his destiny, perhaps baking was Marian's. She was becoming an common name which meant many eyes were watching her. Out of the corner of his eye, he noticed all the young eligible men who were admiring his sister. They were from different families and professions. Placido had confidence that his sister's future suitor could easily come from a wealthy family. His only concern was just how she was going to marry when that seemed to be the one subject she never wanted to think about.

From a broken window at the top of the annexed structure, the masked young man looked down at the ceremony, sitting on a tower of wooden crates. He watched as Marian received the prize for the pie that had conquered all of her competitors once again. She was now going to be the desire of every man in Lucca. The sunlight cascaded down from the cathedral rooftops and in between the angel statues, shining light onto the crowd.

As a young girl placed the golden necklace around Marian's neck, she felt the eyes of the men looking upon her from the crowd. She couldn't resist looking around, recognizing the same men who had admired her many times before. From the cheering crowd, she could hear Placido, whose applause was the loudest of them all. Brightly colored flags with the city's seal were raised throughout the street. The local cathedral bells were ringing, the notes pouring over the cobblestone homes and water fountains of Lucca.

Placido made his way through the crowd to his sister, who was leaving the stage. Opening his arms, he embraced her tightly.

"That necklace looks beautiful on you," he said, walking next to her.

Marian touched the necklace, gazing upon a piece of jewelry finer than any prize she had won before.

"Thank you. The competition was more difficult than last year.

I didn't think I'd win." Marian was flushed, clearly still energized from the award ceremony.

"Marian, you're the best cook and baker in Lucca. I'm not teasing you. It's the truth," Placido said.

"Thank you."

They watched a group of men pass carrying tall wooden poles. Together, they raised the poles, which were connected by banners of brightly colored triangular flags. Artisans began setting up canvas images, preparing for the next festival, which would take place in the center of the town. Across from them, several monks wearing cloaks walked out of the cathedral in a straight line. They sang in their native tongue about God's love and good works.

Placido waved to a passing family and then greeted a few young men he knew with a nod. Marian swiftly moved to his side, hiding from them. Placido shook his head, until he passed by a young woman who caught his attention. He was intrigued by her radiant appearance. In the sun, her blonde hair looked like waves of gold. Her cheeks were flushed like red roses. While he kept walking forward, he turned his head back to look at her, and she did the same. She revealed a timid smile and gripped the fabric of her dress in such a way as to hold his attention. As the woman went along her own way, Placido returned his attention to his sister and noticed she was playing with her necklace, feeling the gold chain with her light fingers.

Placido cleared his throat, noticing two men from a very wealthy family pass by with a nod. They were transfixed and quite bluntly staring at Marian.

"If you marry a wealthy man, you will have more gold necklaces than that of a queen," he said.

"If I had that many, I wouldn't know what to do with them," Marian replied with a shrug of her shoulders.

That afternoon, Marian returned to the annexed building, carrying a small woven basket that held her winning pie. She was curious about the mysterious young man she had met there, despite his surliness. No matter how hard she tried, she could not get him out of her mind. Disobeying his orders, she pushed the doors open, just wide enough for her to fit through, and went inside. Looking around, she saw something quickly move nearby as the doors closed. In the dim lighting of the room, she could not tell what it was. The silence hung over the room, until-

"Why have you returned? I ordered you to stay away."

She turned around to find the young masked man sitting on one of the carousel horses. He faced her, his arms draped around the stallion's long hair, which was decorated with stars. His mask had changed, this time only covering his eyes and the left side of his face. And he was frowning, his thin lips turned downwards.

Taking a deep breath, she finally replied. "I was worried."

"Worried? About me?" he asked utterly confused.

"Yes. About you." Marian stepped towards him carefully. Pulling both ends of her long dress in her hands and leaning forward, she curtsied.

"My name is Marian," she said.

The young man leaned forward, but only slightly.

"My name is Princio."

"Princio…"

"What of it?" he snapped.

"Do you live here? All alone?" she asked glancing around her surroundings.

"I might." Princio leapt off the horse and landed on the floor gracefully.

"The people of Lucca seem to enjoy your baking, Marian. The necklace you are wearing looks familiar to me," he said.

Marian glanced down, touching the gold chain hanging around her neck. She frowned, stroking the chain in between her fingers.

"I was told it is a replica of the necklace the last queen of Lucca wore."

"Lucca had a queen?"

"Yes, several. There's no royal family anymore. The people seem accustomed to living without rule. Is your family related to them?"

"Who?"

"Royalty?"

"No."

Marian frowned. Her eyes glanced over to the seal on his clothing again, as though it were calling for her attention.

"But the seal on your shoulder, it tells me otherwise," she blatantly stated without hesitation.

"My family passed away years ago. We were common folk, living in the countryside on a farm," he explained, snapping at her again.

Marian hesitated, trying to restrain herself from asking more questions even though dozens were still whirling in her head. However, her curiosity overwhelmed her. It felt impossible to stop asking him more. Just like how it felt impossible to avoid staring at his mask. She glanced at him, daring to peek at the way his eyes seemed to stare into hers. Even though his words were often full of venom, his eyes softened after as though he felt guilty for acting as he did. Feeling brave she asked another question.

"So you are alone?"

"Why do you ask?" Princio's eyes narrowed, confused as to why she was so interested in him, a complete stranger.

Marian shook her head, unsure of how to respond.

"No one has cared for me other than my family," he admitted, slowly moving away from her.

Marian skipped forward, following his steps. When he turned around, she stopped.

"I was worried. If you are alone, you could use some company. I brought some of my pie, if you'd like a taste." She pulled the cloth from her basket, revealing several pieces of the pie she spared for him. The aroma thrilled his senses. Tantalizing and sweet.

"Please, have some." She offered gently as though she were trying to sooth a wild beast.

Together they sat on two of the horses, eating her pie in silence. While she ate, Marian often looked over at Princio. Aside from the mask, his habits were fairly normal. She noticed that every time he took a bite, he barely lifted the mask from his face. His eyes seemed to nearly glow in delight from each bite. Even though she had won dozens of contests for her baking, it was watching his reaction that seemed to fill her with the most pride. When they both finished, he smiled deeply before placing the mask firmly back onto his face. Seeing Princio's smile made her smile in response.

"Thank you. It was delicious," he said lowly.

It was the first time she heard a calm tone to his otherwise hostile voice.

"You're welcome. I'm glad you enjoyed it."

She put the rest of the pie back into the basket, covering it with the cloth. Marian stared at Princio's mask, noticing this mask had a rather stoic expression. She kept picturing his true face beneath it and wondered if she'd ever see it again.

"The mask you're wearing is different from the last one you wore," she noted.

"I have several," Princio replied matter-of-factly.

"You do?"

"Come. I'll show you." Princio got up from his seat and walked over to the nearby piles of crates and statues. Marian followed him eagerly, passing the crates towards the other side of the room. The shadows of the statues covered the wall as though there were climbing towards the ceiling to escape. She shook the eerie chill from her body, curious as to where he was leading her. Leaning forward, he opened a narrow door from behind one of the glass mirrors, revealing a narrow hallway that was painted with glorious images of angels and animals. Marian lowered herself, captivated by the paintings that covered the length of the entire hallway. Princio waved his hands, motioning her to follow him. Following close behind, Marian's hands traced over the painted scenery. The smooth colors depicted stories, stories she could easily follow and understand with every step she took. Noticing that the hallway was becoming narrower, she crossed her arms against her chest as she continued walking.

Princio stopped at the entrance of an octagon shaped room, where Marian noticed a makeshift bed, dresser, a large bookcase that reached the ceiling. She saw many used candelabras but it was the wall full of masks that astounded her. From the ceiling, several colored sheets draped down the old walls no doubt covering cracks. She walked over to the wall of masks, drawn by their unique colors and shapes. Each of the masks were shaped and designed to tell their own story through the different styles and designs.

Marian gently drew her fingers across the masks, feeling the smooth ceramic, the thick paint, and soft feathers.

"You have so many," she said with a smile.

"I found most of them here. They must have been worn by those who celebrated with the royal family." Princio observed Marian and his collection from the doorway.

She continued to look at each one, masks for men and women, arranged by their colors and designs.

"I need them," he admitted.

Marian nodded. Using her index finger, she took a quick count.

"*Fifty. Fifty masks...*" she thought to herself, amazed.

Chapter Six

The Palace Portrait

Marian couldn't resist staring at each of the masks, picturing a story for each of them. She could only imagine who the artists responsible for each one could be. It had to have taken great talent to create such faces with quite a imagination to boot.

Princio kept his arms behind his back, standing straight and focused on Marian's expressions. He saw the way her eyes dazzled. Her expression of wonder and awe was nearly breathtaking.

"Have you ever been inside the palace?" Princio asked, watching her.

"No," Marian replied quickly.

He smiled, before nudging her gently. "Come," he said and held out his hand.

Through secret passages and rooms Marian never imagined possible, they wandered from the octagon room into the palace. Opening a door that was inside a wall, they found themselves on a side balcony overlooking the center of the palace.

Lifting up several drapes, Marian looked out and over the thick wooden railing of the balcony. The other palace windows were either boarded up or barely visible, covered in thick dust. The floor looked like a never ending path from one end of the room to the other. Leaning back, she saw an extraordinarily long hallway with several closed doors, next to several tables and painted portraits on the walls.

She followed Princio down the hall, constantly looking over the railing as she walked. At times she feared she'd fall over and thus followed his steps as closely as possible. As she observed a place so very few had ever seen, she noticed that some of the artwork was still untouched. Coming to the steps, which were covered in the same floral print carpet as the hallway, Princio led her through the open space, as though he knew every nook and cranny.

"Sometimes I come here to walk around. I like to imagine the kind of life the royal family and their court lived," Princio admitted.

"It's beautiful," Marian replied, nearly awestruck.

"My grandfather told me stories about this place, but I never thought they were true. All those rooms were occupied by the court and their families. They would feast upon delicious desserts with the king and queen nightly. And then they would all gather round to ride the carousel while their children slept."

"It is fun."

Princio pondered the space. No matter how many times he had wandered the empty halls and desolate rooms, it still felt new to him. He'd always find something he never noticed before and try to imagine what might have happened there all those years ago. As his eyes followed a stray beam of sunlight from a cracked window, he noticed a desk just below one of the large windows mostly covered in ripped drapes. From the natural glow of the outside world his eyes spotted several pieces of parchment and immediately beamed at the sight.

"Hello there." He greeted, making his way over to the desk.

Distracted, Marian's eyes rose to observe the high ceilings that she believed she could never get accustomed to looking at when Princio called her over in a gentle tone.

Lightly trotting over, he lifted the pieces of parchment. "These were drawings made by one of the royal family members. I remember my grandfather telling me about him." Princio explained, lifting the parchment tenderly.

Marian observed the exquisite details, appearing lifelike

without being completely finished. Strokes of lead crafted eyes and eyelashes, strands of hair and this rather solemn expression upon every face. In awe, she pondered that the auctioneers had left them behind. Clearly, they did not believe them to be of any value.

"He drew everyone that lived here. Look, this was me!" Princio exclaimed, handing her the parchment.

She observed three hand drawn faces of the same rather young and lively boy looking in different directions. He looked adorable, with a sense of wonder and curiosity as well as regality. Marian could have sworn she had seen such a face on a porcelain doll not long ago.

"How old were you here?" she asked sweetly.

"I'm not sure. But it must have been right before…we left," he replied, leaning against the desk holding the rest of the drawings.

Marian nodded, looking back at the drawing in silence when she felt Princio's eyes upon her. She glanced back up and noticed he remained frozen on the spot studying her. What Marian failed to notice was that from where she stood, with her feet delicately planted beneath her dress and her hair effortlessly styled she appeared nearly timeless.

"Princio?" she asked in almost a whisper.

"My apologies. It's just…" he stammered unable to complete his thought.

"Perhaps if I knew you then, maybe my family would have had you drawn."

Marian let out a chuckle oblivious to the fact he was abandoning his previous sentence.

"Princio, we both know I would have never been allowed here. Friend or not." She corrected.

"I may not know as much as you about this place but I do know that royals and commoners did not mingle nor should they have to."

"I suppose you are right. Why don't you take a look around? Explore."

Marian raised an eyebrow in silent response.

"Just be careful, some steps might be unsteady."

Marian was hesitant at first, but after handing him the drawings she began to wander the large room without much trouble. Every so often, one of the long, thick curtains would move a little, startling her. She realized that the curtains only moved because of the gentle breeze she created as she passed by.

At first, Marian was startled by the quietest of sounds, only then to be distracted by the items that had been left behind for so many years. She discovered that most of the palace had been emptied, with most of the valuable pieces of art and furniture being sold at the auction. But then she wondered why certain pieces were left behind. She let her fingertips trace along the curved vases and water basins, left to sit in layers of dust. She touched some of the rigid stained glass windows before passing mirrors that would stand from ceiling to floor. She could never imagine living in such a place feeling as small as a mouse in comparison.

Her footsteps echoed throughout the halls, bouncing off the high ceilings. The empty rooms began to blend together. The faint scent of old perfume enticed her at random corners. Her ears tricked her, as sometimes she heard a faint giggle or the clatter of glass and silverware behind her.

Marian turned left and found a spiral metal staircase. Half of the staircase was covered in fallen wood and blocked by a floral pattern cushioned chair. The objects that seemed to frighten her most, however, were the destroyed candelabras at the top of the stairs. She moved the chair and the wood aside, before firmly gripping the metal railing of the staircase. Marian climbed up. There was nothing around her but empty walls, which swirled around her as she climbed. Looking up, she saw a small stained glass window at the center of a ceiling detailing a garden of luscious flowers and long green vines. Reaching the top of the staircase, she almost tripped on the uneven carpet. Marian tried to maneuver around the broken candelabras, afraid to touch them.

As she tried to move off the staircase, one of her hands pulled her back, still gripped onto the metal railing. Marian tugged her hand, wondering why her fingers were locked in place. Taking a breath to prevent herself from panicking, she tugged once more. She eventually broke free, whimpering at the slight pain from the strain. Marian rubbed her hand, bending her fingers until they felt soft again.

Looking back at the uneven carpet, Marian noticed a long drape on the floor that trailed several feet down the hallway. Her eyes followed the drape all the way back to a portrait, which was concealed by the drape. She noticed there were a few slits in the fabric, so that only half of the painting was covered. The man in the painting stared at her coldly with faded eyes. It felt as though he was watching her intently, judging her with malice.

Intimidated by the man's stare, she walked to the drape cautiously and tugged it down with a grunt. The tattered fabric collapsed onto the floor, releasing a cloud of dust into the air that filled her lungs. Marian sneezed and coughed, wildly waving her hands in front of her face. With the drape down, the large portrait was fully revealed before her eyes.

"Princio! Come quick!" Marian called loudly and frantically.

Meanwhile, Princio remained on his knees. He had discovered another mask inside the kitchen, buried beneath a few old dishes that were covered in thick dust. Rough cracks covered both sides of the faded purple plates detailed with gold rim and tiny flowers. The plates screeched in his ears as he carefully shifted them. As he delicately removed the mask, broken pieces of glass scattered onto the floor. He sighed, hating that more items that were left behind were tarnished and broken beyond repair. He held the mask like a mother would a newborn child. The mask was completely black, with tiny moons and stars etched over the eyes. He smiled, looking forward to adding it to his collection.

"Princio! Princio come quick!" Marian's voice called out.

"Marian!" He shouted back and quickly rose to his feet without hesitation.

Princio ran to her as fast as he could, while shouting, "What is it? Thieves?"

"Up here! Come on, hurry!" she called from the spiral staircase.

Princio dashed up the stairs, almost tripping on the uneven carpet and nearly colliding with the candelabras. Reaching the top he found Marian nearby facing a wall.

"What?! What is it?!" he demanded in a rushed breath.

"It's the family portrait," she said almost in a whisper.

Princio stood near to her before the painting. His eyes turned their attention from Marian to the painting and in an instant his mouth dropped open.

"That looks like my mother, my father, and my-" His voice died at the realization of what he was looking at.

"Princio, you're a prince. Royalty," Marian announced looking at him.

"No. No that's not possible." He denied.

Princio took a step backwards and lowered his head. Marian moved closer to him, wanting to place her hands on his shoulders. She could barely hear his mumbles as he rocked his head from side to side.

"This palace is yours," she said with a smile and watery eyes.

"No. No it can't be true..."

Chapter Seven

Growing Up

Marian laid down, resting on the comfortable carpet that she and Princio had cleaned some days ago. She was next to him as he sat uncomfortably on a dark red cushioned chair. Placing her hands on her lap and looking up at the glass ceiling, she let her mind wander. Admiring the vibrant colors, she let her imagination soar. The sharply cut glass reflected light onto the walls around them, like crashing waves of colors. She looked over to Princio, who kept one hand over his forehead and the other around the back of his neck. By his feet was the parchment with his drawn image. His thoughts couldn't wander or soar the way Marian's mind allowed her to do. He kept facing the same wall of reality that had changed his entire life. He felt completely lost.

"To think, all of my life I've been pretending to be someone else. Why didn't my grandfather tell me this? Why didn't anyone tell me?" he thought to himself, confused.

Marian stared at Princio, wondering what he was thinking about. She observed him like a child would a strange animal. She rolled over to her side and put her hands under her head, to use as a cushion. She watched him as he continued to sit in silence. Occasionally, he tapped his foot on the floor in anxiousness. He put his hand over his mouth, muffling his sighs and groans. His eyes kept falling onto the drawing in utter disbelief.

"Princio," she whispered.

He didn't respond, locked in his current position. Ever since he and Marian had discovered the portrait, he had been stiff and tense. She failed to gain his attention repeatedly. Princio was withdrawn and seemed to have no intention in returning to reality. While she knew his mind was just occupied, she couldn't help but feel a little helpless herself. She tried numerous times to help him.

Even though the two of them started to make efforts to clean the palace on their own, it wasn't enough. He'd sweep the floors as if possessed. He clean windows in such an emotionless way that it nearly frightened her.

Frustrated, Marian sighed loudly. She got onto her knees and moved towards Princio slowly. The bottom of her dress dragged slightly against the rough carpet.

"Princio," she repeated, putting her head on his shoulder.

He let out a soft chuckle feeling his heart flutter and heat rise to his cheeks momentarily at the instant closeness between them.

"Yes, Marian?" he asked, trying to feign a small smile.

"Does this mean I have to call you Prince Princio now?" she asked.

He laughed out loud, surprising Marian and himself. It was something he hadn't done in several years. Admittedly his laugh was quite contagious. She could barely prevent herself from laughing in response. At least he was laughing and not yelling at the question she asked.

"That was a serious question," she said, continuing to blush as she watched him laugh.

He was still in the midst of his laughter, clearly distracted when a rather tempting thought provoked her. She waited until he calmed down, before moving her hands towards his mask, hoping to catch another glimpse of the face beneath. Marian gently nudged the mask with her fingers, anticipating some form of resistance. Surprisingly, Princio didn't stop her as she slowly lifted the mask off his face. With this motion she noticed his breathing intensified and one of his feet began to tap violently. When she could almost see his eyes, she felt Princio raise his arms, ready to grab her hands.

"Marian," Princio begged for a moment.

His voice was desperate, like a plea.

"Please? Just this once?" she asked warmly.

Princio stared at her captivating blue eyes from behind the mask and could see this sincerity pooling in her pupils. It made him utterly speechless for reasons he feared he already knew. Marian was the first person since his own family that he had truly become close to. In the short matter of time he knew her, he felt as though he could act as himself, even if that meant still hiding behind masks. He had seen the people of Lucca from the windows. Men, women and children alike living their lives as though time seemed endless. Yet out of all of the women he had observed, none were her. She was different from them in every wonderful way possible.

His fear was still elevated… He took a deep breath and felt as though his heart was going to burst through his chest. His foot tapping hadn't halted. How could he tell her no when she was looking at him with such honesty and compassion?

Princio shut his eyes as the mask was lifted from his face. He stopped tapping his foot. His body tensed. Once again, Marian marveled at the beauty and youthfulness she saw before her. Princio looked nothing like any of the other men she had seen. She believed that if they had seen him they would be envious. He opened his eyes to see Marian looking at him, wearing the same awestruck expression she had the first time they met. His cheeks turned a light shade of red, and his eyes drifted to the floor. He couldn't look at her like that again… He couldn't acknowledge what he was beginning to feel again.

"Can I have my mask back now?"

"No." Marian answered with a whisper.

Hearing her disobey him he questioned, "No? Why?"

"Because you're not hideous. You are not a monster. What will it take for you to believe me?"

He didn't answer her. Marian gritted her teeth in response to his silence. She was growing angry at his actions and couldn't understand why he refused to believe her.

"I will make you believe me," she said firmly. Pulling Princio from the seat, she locked her hands around his arms, dragging him to the nearest mirror she could find.

"Princio, look in the mirror."

"Why?" he asked, suspicious.

"Please?"

Princio sighed and looked at himself in the mirror as she requested. He found himself unable to deny her more and more with each passing day. He saw Marian's reflection on his right, and a young man where he stood. He raised his hands to his face, and the young man in the mirror repeated the action. He touched his smooth skin and thick dark brown hair. He tugged on several hair strands, which moved smoothly between his fingers. Again, the man in the mirror did the same.

Marian sighed, hoping that he was finally waking up watching him observe his own appearance.

"Do you see now? You're not ugly." She reassured calmly.

"Is this really what I look like?" He was unable to remove his hands from his face for fearing if he did then a monster would indeed be there instead.

"It is. You don't need the mask. You're not ugly!" she cried. She forced herself in front of him, hoping that if he could truly see her sincerity he would allow himself to believe it.

Princio shook his head, dazed. It seemed one reveal after another was becoming too much for him to bear. "But, Feletti said-"

"Feletti?" Marian shrieked interrupting him.

"Yes, Feletti. He said I was ugly and that's why I have to wear my masks. And my grandfather! He instructed me to never show my face to anyone. And now...I disobeyed him," he gasped before hanging his head in shame.

As he clasped his hands over his face, a heavy pain filled his chest. Marian slowly raised her hands and placed them on his shoulders. His body shook beneath her hands as she took another step closer to him.

"Your grandfather didn't mean it the way you understood it. Why would your grandfather, who loved you, tell you to hide your face?"

"I don't know! But that is what he told me. With his dying breath, he told me to never show my face. Unless…" Princio's shouting suddenly trailed off, alarming Marian.

"Unless what?" Marian asked. She winced, hiding her face with her hands afraid that he had suddenly become angry with her antics.

Princio didn't reply, trying to understand his own thoughts. Marian lowered her hands and turned away. Her eyes turned back to the stairs and the wall where the portrait was still hanging. Free from the drapes that suffocated it, the painted faces remained nearly immortal. She could feel herself becoming guilty, still grasping the mask and feeling the smooth edges caress her skin. Her heart began to pound as she fought back a few tears. She was trying so hard to help him. She wanted him to understand but didn't know what else to do.

'Perhaps there isn't anything I can do,' she thought. She took a deep breath tightening her grip on the mask. *'No…if he wants it back so badly he'll have to earn it.'* She couldn't give in so easily. Princio is perhaps the first man she felt a connection with and wasn't going to stand by and let him suffer over something that had no merit.

"If you really feel uncomfortable without the mask…here." She held out the mask still gripped in her hands.

Princio reached forward to take it, when she pulled away at the last moment. "Marian," he said while leaning over. His sudden tone woke up a sense of childish joy replacing her sadness instantly. She raised an eyebrow at him and bit her lower lip.

'Yes, if he wants to hide himself from a world he refuses to even see, then he will have to earn it.' She reminded herself with confidence. Taking a step forward she held the mask out again, but pulled it away once he got close enough. She slowly backed away, keeping the mask behind her back where he couldn't reach it. Her small smile turned into a devilish grin. Princio leaned forward, taking one

step towards Marian, becoming increasingly impatient. She however took five steps back.

"Marian. I'm serious," he warned.

Fleeing like a scared animal, Marian let out a loud squeal and rushed to the stairs. Princio quickly followed behind, chasing her up the stairs, down the hall, and all the way back to the carousel constantly calling her name. There, Marian stopped abruptly. She held the mask in front of her in between her fingers, her loose braid hanging over her left shoulder. She waited for Princio to emerge from the door and he did so seconds later, slightly out of breath.

Holding out his hand, he took slow steps towards her trying very hard to keep whatever patience he had left. She moved backward and onto the carousel, trying to hide behind one of the horses.

"Marian, may I please have my mask back?" Princio asked calmly. He followed her, trying to catch his breath. He reached for the mask, which remained clenched within her delicate hands.

"You can have it back…after you catch me!" She ran away hearing Princio sigh in frustration behind her. He chased after her, avoiding the horses and seats unsure as to why she was playing this rather unprovoked game of cat and mouse. She laughed merrily and continued to run away from him, enjoying the thrill of him chasing her. As he tried to catch her, his impatience melted into laughter. Every time Marian looked back, she saw Princio following close behind, laughing. It didn't take long for him to catch up, and soon he cornered her against one of the horses.

He leaned forward nearly close enough that Marian could feel his breath on her face. The sense of being so close to him was nearly overpowering and she only hoped he didn't notice the flush on her cheeks. Princio was tempted to lean forward, just enough for their noses to touch and the ruffled strands of his hair to touch her forehead. He refrained.

"May I please have it back now?" he asked smoothly and calmly.

Marian looked away from him and sighed pretending to be

upset that she lost the game. She used the opportunity to quickly rub her cheeks and try to compose herself.

"If you must," she said. She handed it out to him, ever so slowly. Princio hesitated, waiting for her to trick him yet again. Marian didn't, and before he realized it, the mask was back in his hands.

The next day, the Kingdom of Lucca began preparing for its yearly festival. Throughout the streets, confetti was being made and collected, streamers were being hung from the rooftops, and women were sewing and tying flowers into bouquets and wreaths. Marian and Placido walked among the crowd, watching the Cirque arrive and start setting up for the festival.

As they looked at a table full of food samples, Marian noticed out of the corner of her eye that Feletti was performing nearby. Immediately, she took several steps backwards and hid behind Placido, terrified.

Placido glanced behind him and saw his sister bent downward, hiding and practically clutching hair in between her hands.

Her heart pounded against her chest. She shut her eyes, hoping that Feletti wouldn't see her. From the accordion, a song began to play, grabbing the attention of several children and their parents. Placido noticed Feletti passing by them, playing his tune and briefly making eye contact with a knowing grin. Something about the grin made Placido uneasy. Feletti continued onward and smirked at the sounds of his fans following him from behind.

As Marian remained crouched, she watched Feletti pass in between the gaps of her fingers. Every time she heard his steps, she grew more terrified. She calmed her breathing, staring at his boots, but her fear continued to grow. Suddenly, Feletti's left foot caught a corner of one of the paved stones. He tripped, falling forward. Marian watched as his knee bent inward without breaking. She watched him lean forward, noticing the unnatural movement and shape of his leg.

'What was that?' Marian wondered to herself, trembling.

Feletti stopped and tugged on his upper thigh. He frowned, but forcing himself forward, his knee bending outward again with ease. As he continued to walk, the children followed him, looking for tiny gifts. Once he was out of sight, Placido looked down at his sister and crossed his arms. She remained close to the ground, shocked at what she had just seen. Noticing the shadow that fell over her, Marian looked up.

"We have to talk about this, young lady." Placido was frowning and his eyes were full of concern.

"Talk about what?" Marian asked as she stood up, brushing the dirt off her dress.

"You were hiding behind me again, weren't you?" he asked.

"Yes. So that you would protect me."

With a heavy sigh, Placido put his hand to his forehead. "Marian, I would protect you no matter what. But the thing is, I'm not always going to be-"

"Look!" Marian cried out, pointing to a stand of cultural dresses. She took off, running towards the display. Her eyes were fixed on the vibrant colors and patterns.

"Marian! I'm not done speaking to you," he called after her.

Placido knew that once something else grabbed her attention, Marian was gone. He could only sigh and return to what he was doing.

That night, the preview of the festival music wafted through the warm air. Crisp, clean air swept through the streets and alleyways. Placido's shop closed and the front door was locked. They had made amazing profits today. The shelves were full of newly made toys, waiting to be played with and loved. Placido and Marian could see them from the small dining room, which had not been the same since their father died. The doorway where the giant key once hung was now instead home to a regular door. Placido had given up searching for the thief that had taken it.

Marian retreated to her room right after dinner, avoiding dessert. She had never skipped dessert before. Upon finishing his wonderful meal, Placido let out another sigh. His eyes shifted to the six unopened love letters she had received from potential suitors. All six were fine gentlemen, yet to his dismay, she showed no interest in any of them. He grabbed them before heading towards the wooden stairs to find his stubborn sister. He walked up the steps firmly, turning right onto another set of small stairs. At the top of those small five steps, Placido gently knocked on the closed door of Marian's room, which was engraved with flowers and wings. He received a muffled response from the other side.

Opening the door, Marian's cluttered collection of toys welcomed him. He was always unprepared for the colorful clutter and chaos in his sister's room. Almost every inch of her room, from wall to wall, was covered with the stuffed dolls and toys he had made her. Marian had also collected lace ribbons and garland, which were draped around the door and closed window. Painted angels, flowers, and stars covered the corners of her ceiling. Flower petals were separated by colors and placed in glass vases, which stood on top of the windowsill.

Placido found Marian lying face down on her soft bed, which had the thickest, yet softest, mattress their father could afford. She wrapped her arms around her face. At least the company of her stuffed friends made her feel comfortable.

"Marian," he said quietly.

"Yes?" she asked, her voice muffled against the soft blankets.

"May I please speak with you now?"

Marian sat up, knocking over some of her stuffed toys. She turned to face Placido, who sat at the end of her bed. She noticed the six unopened letters he placed on the bed. Her brother massaged the back of his neck and loosened his shirt before continuing.

"Listen Marian. You may be my little sister now, but one day you will grow up. And though I will always love you, I won't be here forever," he said.

Marian grabbed one of her stuffed bears, dressed in a Roman uniform. Squeezing the bear in her arms for comfort, she took a deep breath.

"Do you understand Marian?"

"Yes," she replied quietly, staring at the letters.

"One day you will be like the other women you see in church. Adorned in flowers at your wedding, with all of Lucca present. Bound to the man who will protect you forever. One day you will be grown up and not...like this." He paused, distracted by the clutter of lace and toys in her room.

"But I like...this." She squeezed the stuffed bear.

"And that's fine. But one day, you will have to grow out of, well, all of this. Did you ever notice the way some of the young men look at you when we're out together?"

Marian shook her head in response.

"I thought not. You're very pretty for your age. You've always been, since you were, well, younger. And the older you grew, the more beautifully you bloomed. You need to grow up and see the world," he said.

Marian looked down, patting the bear on the head. Her eyes were wide and suddenly watery.

"You never opened these," he held up the letters. "You don't know what they say. You don't know what these men are willing to give you as their wife. It could be everything you want."

She refused to make eye contact, nervously staring at the floor.

"I know this is hard for you. You've been gone so much lately; you're clearly avoiding discussing this with me. But, you can't be a child forever."

Placido couldn't have been further from the truth. *There's no way I could tell him about Princio and the carousel now,'* Marian thought, *'He'd never believe me if I did.'*

"Do I live in a fantasy?" she asked, growing more upset. "Am I blind to reality?"

Placido sighed. He gently patted her on her head, trying to keep her from erupting into tears.

"I can't blame you. In a way, I don't want you to grow up yet. You're too much fun." He laughed.

"I'll try to be braver for you. I just...can't when I see Feletti," she admitted.

"Why are you afraid of him?" Placido asked. Deep concern shone in his eyes again. He reached over to hold Marian's hand.

She shifted, imagining Feletti's unsettling expression and the sound of his voice calling her. "I don't know. I just am," she said. Marian squeezed the bear tighter.

"Alright, let's not talk about Feletti anymore. A little while ago, you wanted to talk to me about something. I apologize for being so busy with the shop. The days just seem to blur together. I hope you don't feel neglected."

Marian blinked several times, before shaking her head. "Not at all. It's not important. I actually forgot what it was about."

"If you do remember, I'm here for you." He kissed her forehead and patted her on the head again, making her smile.

As Placido closed Marian's bedroom door behind him he paused thinking of his father and then what Marian confessed to him moments ago. Making his way to his toy shop he decided to spend some time crafting new toys. However, he barely made any progress when a memory long suppressed resurfaced.

He remembered the weeks leading to his father's passing. How spry he looked them. He looked as though death was the farthest thing from him and yet it was slowly taking him. Perhaps there were slight signs but they were all minimal. All the same while Marian was busy baking in the kitchen, completely engulfed in her creation,

Placido's eyes received the revelation and could only look at his father with a near dumbfounded expression.

"Placido?" his father asked, heavy with concern.

"Father your mad...she's-she's not-" Placido stuttered feeling anger rising from his chest.

"She is." His father coldly responded.

"Father-"

"Placido please. I debated telling you this ever since that day and now that I am dying you need to know."

Placido couldn't believe what he was hearing. He was confused and yet found his words very convincing. His father would never lie, never tell such tall tales. And yet why couldn't he believe him?

"Son, you know that I will not recover from this. It doesn't matter how hard I fight. I've made my peace already with God and all I can do now is make sure my children are loved and taken care of. You are all your sister will have left."

"You know I'll take care of her. I always have." Placido responded rather firmly.

Hearing the rather angry tone his father pleaded, "Please don't be angry."

"I'm not angry, I'm in disbelief... Father if what you told me is true then one day Marian-"

"That was the deal." His father interrupted.

Placido nodded, not wishing to talk about this any longer. He tried to shuffle his feet when his father stopped him by gently moving in front of him.

"She must never know Placido. Promise me you will never speak a word of this to her," he ordered with a thick grunt.

Placido nearly rolled his eyes and said exacerbated, "You can't be serious. She has-"

"No," his father interrupted in a cold tone. "She cannot know. Promise me."

Placido reluctantly responded, "I promise."

"Do you?"

"Yes. She will never know."

As Placido's attempts to try and work that evening soon became impossible, Marian fell into a deep sleep like she had many nights before. Snug under her blankets and far from the world she knew, she fell…fell deeper into her slumber unable to hear the faint sounds of music from down the street, unable to hear the sounds of church bells.

Upon opening her eyes she froze in bewilderment at the sight of a glorious ballroom full of dancing couples in costumes and dresses wearing masks. Each pair dancing like perfectly timed toys, with twirls and turns, intertwined and moving with the music.

Taking but one step forward out of anxiousness, Marian noticed she too was dressed like a princess of a kingdom. Her ball gown flowed outward, covering her feet, tied with lace and ribbons. She turned slightly watching the gown move with her and the ribbons in her curled hair twirl around her ears. She hardly had time to process where she might have fell to when she sensed a very familiar presence. Tensing for a brief moment she felt his steps moving towards her from the dancing crowd. Taking a breath, she knew he was coming for her and perhaps for the first time she felt the fear of him vanish. In that one breath she felt unafraid and instead enamored.

With one swift side step, Feletti presented himself before her, dressed like the other gentlemen except he too wasn't wearing a mask. Without speaking and as if on instinct the two began to dance and together they joined the room of masks. Marian could not look away from Feletti, feeling a warmth within her as his hand clasped her delicate one and the other found its place at her waist.

She moved fluidly as if she had known this dance all her life. The music made her feel lighter than air as her heart began to swell. Her face flushed a delightful shade of pink and every time her eyes fell on

Feletti, she felt that warmth spread throughout her. He never once broke eye contact with her as he moved impeccably.

Holding her close for a brief moment, face barely touching hers, he finally spoke. "This can be your future. A waltz. A beautiful gown. Endless elegance."

Marian absorbed what he said but felt her warmth beginning to fade.

"I know you desire what once was and this can be yours. This world can be once again." He whispered into her ear.

Marian felt the chill from his words and kept herself composed. Feletti twirled her twice and held her even closer than before. Marian felt as though she recognized his possessive nature.

"I shouldn't have let you go. I see that now. And I want to give you everything you want." He explained deeply.

Finding her voice Marian replied, "What if this isn't what I want?"

Feletti frowned and looked at her confused. She slowly began to stop dancing with him, noticing how the other couples remained oblivious to their presence.

She repeated, "What if this isn't what I want?"

"Then tell me what it is you want and you can have it," he answered firmly.

She shook her head and countered, "You can never give me what I want."

Instead of scowling or leaving her on the dance floor he instead held her close and explained, "Yes I can. I can do so much more than you are even aware of. Including getting you to change your mind."

Marian pulled away and suddenly the room became black as if a giant shadow encased the room. Alone in the darkness Marian felt the ground beneath her buckle and she fell...

Her eyes barely opened, unable to see her door behind all of her blankets bunched in her tight grip. She blinked a few times, her heart still racing, however she refused to acknowledge she was still scared.

The dream had taken a turn she never expected. While Feletti haunted her days she hoped he'd be forbidden from her dreams, but it seems he wasn't. However the last thing she wanted to do was dwell on him another second. Not when she was looking forward to seeing Princio.

Chapter Eight

Feletti's Dream Dolls

Marian took a deep breath, shutting her eyes and raising her arms in the air. When she opened her eyes, she smiled. The displays were finally coming together. Even with the recently cloudy weather, the people were still enjoying their usual outings. They were out and about, spending time with their families and the festivities, while also enjoying delicious food together. She turned around, looking for Princio. As usual, she found him hiding in the shadows.

"Princio? Come," she called. She actually stomped her foot, growing impatient. Marian didn't hear or see him. A moment later, she saw him come out of the darkness.

Princio craned his neck forward, looking around while he moved slowly towards Marian.

"You'll be fine. Trust me." Marian gave him a reassuring smile.

Princio walked over and stood next to her, holding one of his masks. He firmly pressed the mask on his face, making sure it would not fall off. His shiny, somewhat greasy hair was pushed back behind his ears, with some of the wavy strands hanging over his forehead.

"Princio," Marian looked at him, pouting slightly. "Must you wear your mask in public?"

"Yes," he replied.

"At least no one will find it peculiar. Not until the Cirque leaves..." She grabbed his arm, leading him into the Kingdom of Lucca for the first time.

"You haven't left the building since you came back?" Marian asked, looking at him.

"I've watched this kingdom from the windows. I've observed Lucca at its finest. It's very different from where I was living." Princio's eyes lingered on everything they passed by.

"What was it like?"

"Different. I lived north of here, on a farm. We could see distant towns over the hills and down the valleys. It was just me and my grandfather after my parents died."

He paused to look up at the sky, enjoying the warmth of the sun. Some time had passed since he had last felt it on his skin.

A few people walked towards them, nodding and smiling as they passed. Marian nodded. She was relieved that they did not question whom she was with. They all looked at Princio like he was one of their own.

"Don't you like Lucca?" she asked. Marian looked down and watched their feet as they walked together in unison.

"Well, it's different. Although, yes, I do like it here. But..." He hesitated, stopping near a stand full of paper dolls for children.

Marian moved to his side, noticing the sadness in his eyes behind the ceramic texture of his mask.

"What is it?" she whispered.

"If my parents ruled Lucca and suddenly left, why doesn't anyone seem to miss them? Were they terrible people?" He stared at the king and queen paper dolls, which were sitting in paper thrones. They wore bright smiles with rosy cheeks, and crowns rested upon their holy heads. The two dolls were also holding hands.

Marian bit down on her lip gently, looking at the same paper dolls. She watched as Princio touched them gently, before touching the other paper dolls placed around the king and queen. His eyes fell upon the couples and their children, all dressed in fancy clothing.

"I'm afraid you're asking the wrong person. I don't know

much about them. But I have a strong feeling they were loved," she said.

Princio smiled at her response. At times, he looked over at Marian, starting to notice little things about her that he did not see before. The way she smiled. The way her eyes almost seemed to glow with happiness. As they walked, he glanced down and saw that her hands were awfully pale. However, the rest of her complexion was the same, peachy white. He also noticed the looks Marian received from several men. The men glanced back at her discretely, observing her beauty like gentlemen.

As they passed several acrobats who were giving preview performances, the two came to a display for Feletti, which read: "Feletti's Dream Dolls Shop." Marian's feet suddenly froze and her heart began to beat wildly. She slowly backed away from the giant canvas, which had a painted image of Feletti on it. Princio turned around and saw Marian backing away, who seemed unable to take her eyes off the painted canvas.

"I don't like that man," she whispered.

"Feletti?"

"He owns a doll shop. Calls them dream dolls. It is rumored that he does favors for others at a price. If you can even call them favors," she said bitterly.

"I've never seen his shop but he's told me about it. He was my first friend when I arrived."

"Feletti is not a friend," Marian corrected sharply.

"Why do you say that?" Princio asked. He stared at her, baffled. Feletti had been nothing but kind and helpful to him since he had arrived.

"He gives me a cold feeling that won't go away. He makes me sick and frightened. He is always playing that eerie music." Marian rubbed her arms up and down. The mere thought of him gave her chills.

'Everything about him is wrong,' she asserted to herself.

Princio remained silent, unsure of how to respond. He held back his desire to defend Feletti, unwilling to upset Marian further.

Instead, he looked down at the canvas and the small stand, which had a painted arrow pointing to Feletti's shop. Fixing his mask, he started walking in that direction.

"You said Feletti does favors, right? Do you think he can help out a friend?" Princio asked.

"No, Princio don't," Marian warned.

"I want to take a look at his shop. See what keeps him so busy," he said, taking large steps towards the shop.

"No Princio!" Marian called after him, shouting. His steps slowed as he reached a small dip in the road.

"What's the harm Marian? He's probably not even there."

"NO! Please! Let's go back," she begged Princio, shrieking wildly.

As Marian's eyes swelled with tears, Princio stopped. He slowly turned around. Marian was unlike he'd ever seen her before. She was distressed and frightened to the point that her voice was cracking.

'Why is she this terrified of him?' Princio wondered to himself.

"Please Princio, let's go back," she repeated.

"Alright," he sighed. "Let's go back. It looks like it might rain actually." He glanced up only for a second, noticing the thin layer of clouds which were suddenly crawling over the tops of the shops. Marian let out a strange laugh, mingled with gratitude and relief.

From around the corner, Feletti listened carefully. He kept himself steady and firm against the stone wall, silent as a graveyard. Feletti had recently left his shop to search for future customers. He turned his head to the side, far beyond what was natural for other people, watching Marian's and Princio's backs as they walked away. He didn't smile, but he felt deeply satisfied about what he had just overheard.

Chapter Nine

Chains of Friendship

Princio woke up the next morning, his back aching. He had slept restlessly all night. News of heavy rains from the north had swept throughout the kingdom. Thick grey clouds were arriving. Rain was imminent. The working men of Lucca had commandeered his annex, spending hours setting up several displays and sets for the Cirque, safely inside. He had been forced to remain hidden in his room, through the secret passage. Thankfully, as the workers set up the festival displays, they did not acknowledge the large carousel in the back of the room. He was relieved when they finally left, allowing him to move freely about the annex once more.

After stretching out on his back, he grabbed some food that Marian had made for him the day before. He opened one of the brightly colored bags to discover a baked pomegranate pie. He inhaled the sweet scent and his mouth started watering. Finding a note underneath the pie, he read it, laughing at her promise that she'd be back with an onion dish.

"Should I have this pie for breakfast?" he pondered aloud. He grinned, grabbing the pie. "I am a prince after all. And I do…what I want." He laughed. Holding the pie in his hands, he turned around and saw Feletti sitting on one of the crates, smiling at him from underneath his hat.

"Good Lord!" Princio yelled. He nearly dropped the pie onto

the floor. "Feletti, you scared me," he said. Princio tried to put the pie down without dropping it, shaking slightly. He looked for his plate and utensils among his other belongings, which were scattered about the room.

"Hello Princio. Long time no see, my friend," Feletti greeted him.

"Yes. It has been. I'm glad to see you again."

"I do apologize. I've just been so busy with my shop. So many people to please. I hardly have any time to enjoy myself anymore."

"I'm surprised you don't mention your shop more often. I didn't know you were so popular in Lucca," Princio said while sitting down.

"Well it's not like you were going to visit anytime soon. You must remain here, remember? Where you are safe. Where no one can see you." Feletti tilted his head to the side, craning his neck. He grunted for a moment, feeling his head and neck lock. He tugged at his head for a moment, feeling the lock loosen. He twisted his head all the way around, finally feeling comfortable again. Princio cut a large piece of the pie for himself, oblivious to his friend's struggle.

"Someone told me that you do favors for others. I was hoping, maybe, you could do a favor for me."

"Who told you?" Feletti asked, facing the wall.

"Marian."

Feletti turned to face Princio. He glared down at the slice of pie Princio was about to eat. "Who made you that?" he asked through gritted teeth.

"Marian. She's a wonderful baker," Princio answered, smiling.

"So I've heard."

"Would you like some?"

"No, thank you. I don't eat breakfast," Feletti replied, practically sneering at the juicy pie. He tried to sit more comfortably, crossing his long legs and fixing his hat upon his rough hair. "I am a little lost Princio. I haven't seen you in a while. Let us backtrack, yes? How did Marian find you?"

"She found the key to the carousel," Princio said with a shrug.

"SHE WHAT?" he screeched.

Feletti leaped onto the carousel. He saw for himself that the large wooden key was inside the blue lock. He glared at the key, his eyes narrowed in disbelief.

"Where did she find this?" Feletti asked, touching the key. His voice was strained, struggling to remain composed.

Princio stared at the key. He lowered his voice to calm his friend. "Marian said there was an auction of some of the palace items. Her brother-"

"Placido," Feletti interrupted.

"Yes, he bought it." Princio was surprised by Feletti's tone of voice.

"I see…"

"She found me asleep on the carousel. She…she saw me. She… saw my face…"

"Yes, and I see it too," Feletti chuckled.

"No. Feletti, she saw my real face."

Silence fell between them. Feletti tried to comprehend what he had just heard. "Not your mask?"

"Correct."

Feletti hesitated. His eyes were beginning to tighten so much that they began to crack around the corners.

"I also came across a discovery," Princio said calmly.

"Really? And that is?" Feletti asked, slowly walking away from Princio's line of sight. He could feel the chambers in his chest beginning to burn as his temper began to flare.

"I don't think I need to remain within these walls alone anymore."

Feletti snapped one of his fingers in half. His lips were firm and tight as he asked, trembling with anger, "How so?"

"It seems as long as I wear my mask, no one will see my face. Except for Marian."

"That is true," Feletti replied, snapping his finger back in place.

"And you'll never believe this but…I'm a prince."

Feletti's frown twisted into a smile on his mouth, which widened and grew.

"Excuse me?" he asked, breaking another finger out of Princio's sight.

"I am a prince. My parents were the king and queen of Lucca, and yet my grandfather never told me. I can't believe it myself. The palace is truly my home," he exclaimed, smiling cheerfully. Princio shook his head, still surprised at this discovery. He placed a hand on his mouth before continuing.

"If Marian hadn't found the portrait..."

"Yes. How fortunate," Feletti interrupted. Annoyed, he put his fingers back in place. "She seems to make you happy. You smile. You never used to smile."

"Marian says I'm handsome. The first person who had told me that. She says that I don't need to wear the masks," he added.

Feletti's anger grew. He shook from side to side as he stood. The cracks around his eyes were becoming deeper, splintering like wood. Princio continued, oblivious to his friend's anger.

"She's so kind, telling me that I am handsome when I am actually grotesque. Just thinking about her now, I miss her."

"Really?" Feletti folded his hands close to his face, suddenly intrigued.

Princio nodded.

"She's changed my life in ways I never thought possible."

"So, from my understanding, Marian is an important person to you."

"Yes. She is."

'What an inconvenience,' Feletti thought.

Princio returned to his pie, savoring each bite.

"This pie is so good! Feletti, are you sure?" He held out the pie. Feletti shook his head, fighting the urge to spit at it.

"Oh no. Thank you, friend. But I cannot. To think that I was worried, so worried that you would be lonely without me, while 'Marian' has actually been keeping you company. To think that I was trying to protect you from the cruel people in Lucca, and yet you converse with them. To think I call you my 'friend,' and yet you don't seem to care about my thoughts," Feletti said with growing anger.

Princio frowned, hearing his friend move towards the nearest tower of boxes. "Are you upset Feletti?"

"Oh, don't you worry about me. I wish I could stay, but I must return to my shop. So many customers, so little time." Feletti leapt off the tower, landing perfectly on his feet. Princio's head whipped around to find Feletti standing on the marble floor, leaning on one of the posing statues. He glanced at the elegant pose of the statue, nearly tempted to push it over to watch the beautiful marble body shatter onto the floor.

'After all, it is Marian you should be worried about,' Feletti thought, while straightening the bent brim around the front of his hat.

"Feletti, wait! Before you go. Could you at least consider helping me?" Princio asked.

Feletti's sly grin returned to his face. "What kind of 'help' were you thinking of?"

"I don't know what kind of help you provide, but I've been thinking. I really want to see my parents again. I don't know if you can…"

"Oh well, that's something I haven't done in a long time." Feletti pondered as he glanced at the statue's timeless face, immediately recalling the last time he had done so. "Yes. I will pull some strings and see what I can come up with. But really, your parents? Whatever for?"

Feletti walked towards Princio with his hands behind his back, taking calculating steps. His feet clicked and clacked across the spotless floor, echoing about the room.

Princio hesitated before explaining, unsure if this was indeed what he wanted. "Since they died when I was so young, it would be nice to see them, at least once. I feel the need to confide in them. Especially now that I know I am the prince of Lucca."

"Interesting, since they are most likely to blame for your grotesque face." Feletti reminded cruelly, tapping Princio's mask with his index finger.

His sentiment rattled Princio.

"Am I? Am I truly grotesque?" he asked, bowing his head.

"Of course you are. Don't you think Marian only tells you otherwise because of the kindness of her heart?" Feletti rolled his eyes, carelessly moving about to another statue posed as though it were ready to welcome him into it's arms. "She's lying to you. You must have suspected as much."

Glancing over at Princio, he noticed his weakened eyes and tutted. "Truly you amaze me Princio. It seems I underestimated how foolish you can be. Did you really think she would-"

"Enough." Princio boldly snapped with a glare.

Feletti smirked crookedly, glancing at the statue and staring into it's eyes full of longing.

"But never mind her. I promise I'll be back soon with your answer. Marian...may be helpful. But I wouldn't want to lead you astray."

Hearing this filled Princio with hope. It wasn't a promise but it was a promise to try.

"Thank you Feletti. You are a true friend. I am in your debt." Princio gave him a bow of thanks.

"It is no trouble at all, your highness." Feletti replied, bowing to him.

'I think I know how you can repay me,' he thought, grinning as he walked away.

Chapter Ten

Feletti's Favors

Whenever she saw or heard Feletti, Marian couldn't stop chills from running through her body. The pounding of her heart rattled her chest. She heard his twisted music almost every day. Playing in her ears over and over again, like some form of punishment. Slowly blinking her heavy eyelids and wrapping her face in the comfort of her arms, Marian looked at the portrait of herself and Placido when they were younger. The portrait sat on her small nightstand, in an old frame decorated with her favorite accessories. Though she remembered her father, she had more memories with Placido. His advice to her about being brave was nothing surprising. She never doubted him, knowing he was better than any hired tutor money could pay for.

Marian considered how to be brave. Feletti was her only fear, her only source of terror. Taking a deep breath, she decided to see Feletti's doll shop for herself, and to find out what kind of favors he performed. She waited until Placido retreated to his workshop, before leaving the shop undetected.

She ventured towards the shop alone. The streets were becoming empty, as it was almost time for the sun to set. People were returning home to their families to eat their dinners. She could smell the faint scents of homemade sauces and gravy wafting from the chimneys and open windows. The sounds of utensils being pulled from oak drawers and seats being moved could also be heard from nearly every home. Following the same path she and Princio had taken the other day, Marian went down the slightly sloped cobblestone road. She noticed a man who was just ahead of her, walking in the same direction as the shop.

Marian watched the man as he came to the front of Feletti's shop, entering by gently pushing the door open. She hesitated before deciding to pursue him. The shop was oddly placed within a brick wall. There were no homes or businesses surrounding it, and the front was nothing but a large bay window. The door was simply glass, with black trimming that was starting to peel off. Coming closer to the window, she bent down and peered over the windowsill. Marian immediately recognized some of the dolls displayed. She looked at them, still on her knees, keeping her hands steady by clinging onto the thin windowsill. Examining the dolls, she faintly recognized two fairy dolls with lavender and gold wings, and the soldier that always protected them.

Inside she could see the man sit down at a table across from Feletti. She looked past the dolls, unable to hear their conversation. They sat at a rounded table, which was near the back of the room underneath several lit candelabras that casted large shadows onto the plain walls. Most of the shelves were not leveled, and were draped with some kind of black lace. She noticed that there were two shut doors to the left, each decorated with a door knocker shaped into some kind of unidentifiable creature.

"My son wants a puppy in the worst way. But only those who belong to high society know where to find them, and also afford them. I'm a carpenter. Although I love my work, it's not enough. I don't want to fail him. I have failed him many times before." The carpenter rested his elbows on the table and sighed deeply.

"Of course. What kind of father would you be, if you are unable to deliver?" Feletti leaned forward, his hands folded near his mouth.

"Will you be able to help me?" the carpenter asked.

"Of course I can help you. Let me see," Feletti looked at his shelves, searching for puppy dolls. His eyes scanned the few dolls he had, before finally choosing a suitable one. Feletti stood up and took the doll from the shelf. The doll looked brand new. There wasn't a single speck of dust on its small, cupped ears. The light yellow fur had been brushed, and it was soft to the touch. Black beads were used for almost every feature of the doll, from the eyes, to the nails, and even the outline of its pink paw pads. The doll rested perfectly in between Feletti's arm, sewn into a seated position, with its long and bushy tail curled against its hind legs.

"This doll is an exact replica of the same dog that belonged to the last royal family in Naples. This breed is a family dog, and one that your son will love forever." Feletti instructed the carpenter to close his eyes. Tenderly, Feletti took off his gloves, one and at a time, revealing that his hands were made of wood. He took the doll and pulled strange thread out of his coat pockets, sewing it around the ears and tail. Feletti mumbled to himself while he tied a dark blue ribbon around the doll's neck. The entire room darkened as the candle flames flickered wildly. Finishing, Feletti stood up and placed his gloves back onto his hands. The candles lit the room again.

"He is done."

The man opened his eyes and saw the puppy, ready to be taken home in its doll form.

"Thank you, Feletti. Thank you!" he screamed with joy.

Feletti nodded, wearing a wicked grin on his face.

Raising a finger in the air he warned, "Remember, do not present the doll until tomorrow afternoon. Keep it somewhere safe until then." Feletti looked at the grandfather clock to check the time. He stared at the glass, watching his reflection as he adjusted his gloves on his hands. In the reflection, he could see someone watching from the window. When he focused on the image, he recognized Marian's face in the corner. He grinned, before fixing the brim of his hat.

"The payment I request is this: that upon the moment of my choosing, the dog becomes a doll again and returns home."

"Yes, yes, of course," the carpenter agreed absentmindedly,

distracted by the new puppy. He could hardly wait to see the look on his son's face.

Feletti looked up at Marian again with devious intent. Marian's eyes widened as she and Feletti made eye contact. She rose to her feet in a panic, almost tripping as she ran away, moving as fast as she could.

"Wonderful," Feletti said to himself, chuckling.

Chapter Eleven

The Truth

What Marian had witnessed at the shop haunted her all night and into the next day. Every time she recalled Feletti's wooden hands, she became terrified all over again. She was so paralyzed with fear that she barely spoke during breakfast. Placido was also silent, preoccupied with the sudden lack of customers. Her memory of Feletti and the doll troubled Marian so much, that every time she visited Princio afterwards, she couldn't find any joy in seeing him. She felt constantly surrounded by Feletti's presence. With each step, she could feel him following close behind.

Princio sat on the throne where his father, the king, once sat. He laid his arms on top of the armrests and rested his head gently on the back of the throne. Princio imagined a room full of friends. Marian sat on her knees next to him, enjoying a hand drawn book that contained pictures of palaces and exotic animals. The room itself was a giant, empty space. The floor was adorned with small holes and covers, where hot coals were placed for heat during the cold seasons. A large red carpet with floral patterns stretched all the way from the throne to the door and down the next three hallways. The walls, which had once been painted in a lush blue and green, had long since faded. Each glass window had a small stained glass image. Although they had made great efforts to clean and restore the palace to the best of their ability, it wasn't enough. It felt like an unending task but one he'd happily continue with Marian by his side.

Princio looked at Marian, noticing her unusual behavior. She flipped through the pages of the book as though she was just passing time, not for enjoyment. He missed her joyous smile.

"Marian? What's wrong?" he asked concerned.

"Nothing," she replied, turning another page.

"It can't be nothing. Haven't you noticed? I'm not wearing a mask. That should make you smile, yes?"

She closed the book in her lap slowly. Her fingers tugged at the spine, tied together with thick rope and twine.

"I'm sorry Princio. I guess I'm…not feeling that well today," she excused.

Marian looked up and saw his handsome face, which made her stomach flip and flutter. She had been so lost within her own anxieties that she didn't notice. She swallowed thickly, unsure what to do about the sensations in her stomach.

"You did this for me?" she asked.

"Of course I did."

His response made her smile. Settling into the throne more comfortably, he looked around at the empty space. He had imagined how lively this room would have been. He imagined foreign royal families paying visits with a plethora of gifts. He pondered how he must have looked as a child, with no concept of how important his parents were to the kingdom.

"Marian, do you know what happened to my parents?" he asked suddenly.

"From what the story says, a plague was spreading throughout several cities south of Lucca. The king and queen were afraid of dying, so they left with their court. They traveled northward to Brescia, where it is believed they caught the plague and died. The plague never reached Lucca. The king's father raised their only child, the prince. Everyone believed the royal family abandoned them. Once the plague passed, only a select few entered the palace. But since then, it has remained abandoned. The people have been living happily in a democracy since," Marian explained in detail.

"My grandfather raised me, told me stories about Lucca, but I never believed them to be true. I always assumed Brescia was my home. As he lay dying, he told me to return to Lucca and hide my face."

With a heavy sigh, Princio continued. "I remember sitting under a tree with my grandfather and his books. He taught me everything he knew. He seemed so knowledgeable. But I always assumed that his stories were only dreams. I had assumed my memories were dreams. Like this bright blue and green outfit that was displayed on a bed, with shoes to match. An orchestra that played music while couples passed by, with drinks in their hands. Children dressed in suits and gowns next to their parents."

"But you don't remember your parents? Sitting on your father's lap, or being held by your mother?"

"No. I do feel, however, that they were very affectionate to me." He stopped talking, unable to remember more. He faked a smile, touching Marian's chin gently with his hand. Marian was immediately soothed by his touch. She desired more of his affection. But was it foolish to want such a thing? Would an actual prince want to be with someone like her, of no royal blood or birthright? She needed to ignore those fantasies and focus on what she knew was real.

"A beautiful lady like yourself should not be on her knees before the prince, but at his side," he stated with a hint of authority.

Marian saw the empty seat next to him, the very throne where the queen once sat.

"Please, sit." He offered. His open palm graced the seat next to him.

"I can't. I'm not royalty," she argued, feeling intimidated by such an object meant only for royals. If his parents were still alive to see this they'd be fit to be tied.

"As prince of Lucca, I give you permission to sit beside me."

"Princio," she started to protest. "I can't. I'm not allowed to."

"If you refuse to sit because of tradition, be my queen."

"Pardon...me?" Marian choked.

Princio leaned forward and touched her cheek, brushing his thumb across her soft skin. Marian's heartbeat quickened and she could feel her the room start to spin.

With a tone she never heard leave his lips he replied, "Be my queen. Stay with me."

Marian couldn't find her voice, stunned by his words. She didn't know how to respond. Was she wrong about her fantasies? Was she truly correct about his feeling all along? Her lips began to quiver.

"Princio, I really have to be going before Placido starts worrying about me." She quickly stood up, almost falling forward.

"Marian…"

"I'm sorry I can't stay longer. He's been a little down. Perhaps I could bake him something to cheer him up."

Princio snatched her hand and felt its unusual coldness. He squeezed it, trying to apply warmth. The sensation struck him as odd.

"Marian, your hands are cold," he said confused. Princio gently moved his fingers up and down her hand. Marian watched as he touched her knuckles, and then looked at to her with a frown.

"Nothing a little baking can't warm. I'll be fine," she said, replying quickly in the hopes he'd let her go.

Princio's frown remained, wanting to lock his fingers within hers. He attempted to do so, only to feel her pull away. He cleared his throat. With a saddened voice, he said, "Be careful. See you tomorrow?"

Marian smiled, squeezing his hand reassuringly. "Of course, your majesty."

Princio watched Marian pick up the bottom of her dress so she could run down the long carpet, leaving the book behind by his feet. She quickly disappeared around a corner, taking a quick passage outside.

Marian felt the cold breeze whip at her face and wrapped her shawl tighter around her. It was another day without any sunshine. She quickened her pace, wanting to go home as soon as she could. She couldn't bear keeping Princio a secret any longer. She couldn't hide him from Placido any longer. If Princio meant every word he had said, then her brother deserved to know. She felt guilty deceiving him about how she was spending her days, and with the prince of Lucca no less. The only thought on her mind was getting home and speaking to Placido immediately.

As she hurried along, she heard the sound of a puppy barking nearby. She slowed her steps and glanced over a vegetable cart filled with fresh produce. Turning around, she saw a small child playing with an adorable puppy. She watched as the father handed the well-fed pet to his eager son.

The dangling dark blue ribbon caught her eyes, stopping her breath. Marian felt a cold chill run down her spine. Her legs started to shake. She turned around to run home, when she gasped aloud. Behind her, Feletti was already waiting.

"Marian. Like my work?" he asked calmly.

She didn't answer him. Her heart continued to beat rapidly. It pounded so loudly she could hear it inside her ears.

"You've been watching me lately, haven't you?" He took a small step towards her. He smiled gently, stroking her cheek with the back of his glove covered hand. Marian remained frozen with terror.

"I always knew you had a curious streak in you. You always wandered from the table to your seat at the window," he explained, thrilled by her fear.

Marian didn't reply, but remained still against the stone wall, unable to move away from him.

"It was your personality that intrigued me. You became my favorite. My favorite amongst them all."

He stared at her, listening to her panicked breaths. "Do you understand why you fear the music I play?"

Marian didn't respond. She began to weep bitterly. He leaned forward to whisper in her ear.

"That was the music you heard while I was creating you."

Marian's eyes tightened with confusion. Feletti put both of his arms around her, trapping her against the wall.

"It's time you come home with me," he said. Engulfed in his shadow, everything went black for Marian.

Chapter Twelve

Missing

Princio began to worry. Ever since he had asked her to stay with him, he hadn't seen or heard from Marian. While looking out his windows, he couldn't find her anywhere. Being away from Marian, being unable to see or talk to her, made Princio sick. He lost his appetite for food and couldn't fall asleep at night. It was unlike her not to return.

He had become so accustomed to her company in such a short amount of time. It baffled him how their unlikely friendship was growing into something more. It was such an unexpected transformation and yet…what if she didn't feel such things for him? What if that is why she refused to return? He paced by his bed, unsure what to do.

Tired of waiting and tired of suffering, he decided to wander Lucca alone. He'd never thought to be in a position such as this but he had no choice. He ventured on his own, wearing one of his masks for protection. Princio passed many people, but everywhere he looked, there were no signs of Marian. Many nodded and smiled at him, dressed in costumes and masks, hands full of treats and savory dishes. Every time someone acknowledged him, he would panic for a moment, before letting out a sigh of relief when he was not forced into unwanted conversations.

He wondered where to search for help. He knew Marian was

popular, at least in terms of her baking and beauty but still…he didn't know whom to ask. Who would know her the best? Looking at the shops and reading each of their names aloud he suddenly remembered an important detail.

'Marian said her brother owned a toy shop. Her brother Placido.'

Shop after shop, he read the names that were painted and engraved onto wooden signs. Often times he'd stare from the windows, desperately searching for even a trace of Marian. Ahead of him, Princio finally saw the name Placido on the sign of a toy shop.

'This must be it,' he thought.

He entered the shop and was greeted by the fresh smell of wood and a roaring fire. Stepping onto the hardwood floor, he found Placido, who was working on a wooden Roman soldier in the back of the room. He was gently bolting the arms together so they could bend forwards and backwards with a gentle push. In the light Princio could see that his eyes were watering. The entire shop was lit with candles and filled with the fumes of strong wine. Princio noticed two empty wine bottles next to broken glasses that hadn't been picked up.

"Excuse…pardon me, kind toy maker," Princio said awkwardly, unsure how to approach the toy maker. He cautiously took a few steps forward, hearing the floor creak beneath his boots.

Placido looked up from his work. He turned to find a young man wearing a strange, decorative mask. He didn't let the stranger's appearance distract him.

"Ah yes, what can I do for you?" Placido asked, wiping his nose quickly and clearing his throat.

"I was hoping you could tell your sister that I'd like to see her, please."

Placido stopped working on the toy instantly. He placed both of his hands against the wooden table, lifting himself up slowly and silently. He breathed deeply, before letting out a loud grunt and grabbing the wooden mallet. Looking down at the toy soldier, he hesitated, before throwing the mallet in a fit of rage towards a shelf of wood shavings across the room.

Princio winced at the loud bang, terrified by his sudden change in behavior. Stuttering, Placido tried to speak.

"She, she-"

Princio interrupted eagerly. "Yes? Marian? Where is she?"

"I don't know where she is. She's been missing for a week now." Placido explained, almost in tears.

"What?" Princio gasped. She couldn't have been missing, could she?

"She never came home. No one has seen her. No one knows where she is."

"This can't…where was she last?" Princio asked, shocked.

"Marian told me she was buying bread for the linguini dinner. But…no one saw her at the bakery." He took a deep breath, trying to compose himself. "I'm at my wits end. Good Lord, I want her back." Placido wept, putting a hand over his forehead and then over his eyes.

"I'll find her." Princio announced, walking towards the door.

"You won't," Placido eerily admitted.

Princio paused and turned to face the toy maker as he attempted to clean up the empty wine bottles and broken glass.

"If she is where I think she is, it's too late."

"Where?"

"My father made a deal out of desperation and foolishness. He should have known better but then again…if he hadn't, this world wouldn't have been nearly as bright."

"Placido, where is she?"

"No one can find her. Don't you understand that? No one will." Placido spoke as if he was warning the young masked man before him.

"Marian is my sister and I'm supposed to protect her. But she's more than that. She's not just my sister…"

Princio left the shop refusing to hear anymore of his heartbreaking words. He was determined to find her, and he wouldn't stop until she was in his arms.

Chapter Thirteen

The Doll's House

Marian's eyes fluttered open. Sitting up, she saw that she had been lying upon a dark pink carpeted floor. Turning her head, she spotted several abandoned carriages and displays from the Cirque. The grand carousel was resting quietly on the other side of the room. Noticing the covered statues, Marian realized she was back at the annexed building next to the palace, Princio's home.

'*The carousel? But why am I...here?*' Marian asked herself.

Marian looked around the room, which was shaped like a box. The room was so small that she could touch the ceiling with her hands. One wall was glass, through which she had recognized the annexed building. She leaned against one of the other, rose bud painted walls, scratching at it like a trapped cat. Pushing up against the ceiling, she found that it wouldn't budge, no matter how hard she tried. Marian crawled over to the other end of the room, where she discovered a rounded door. Taking a deep breath, she slammed herself into it. She yipped, her shoulder burning with pain. Rubbing her shoulder, she noticed that it felt stiffer than usual. She continued to rub her shoulder, before realizing that her other shoulder was growing numb.

Panicked, Marian tried to calm herself down. She quickly scanned her surroundings. Pillows cross-stitched with the images of lambs and flowers surrounded two of the four corners of the room.

There was also a small bed, an unlit candelabrum, and an elaborate tea set placed upon a small table. All the items in the room were familiar. Marian started rubbing her arms, wondering why she recognized everything in the room. Her deep blue eyes looked out the glass window again, and she began to rock herself from side to side.

'Where am I?' she wondered to herself.

She moved closer to the window, looking around when she suddenly saw Princio at the left corner of the room. Hanging his head and dragging his feet, he entered the room with an expression full of pure heartbreak. He stopped near the small room Marian was trapped in. She watched as he looked about the abandoned carriages and then gazing upward, as though he were looking for something. His light brown eyes were narrowed with frustration.

Marian's heart began to pound as she quickly crawled towards the glass. Pushing her hands flat against the cool surface, she heard it rattle. She began slamming her hands against it. With each punch and push she heard the sound of the glass rattle grow louder, but it didn't break. The glass remained unscathed.

A dull noise nearby alarmed Princio, distracting him from his thoughts. He had tried and failed to find Marian but deemed it useless as the sun began to set. He would continue his search tomorrow but his hope was beginning to wane. Upon finding the source of the sound his eyes lit up. He found Marian trapped within a box upon a cart, wearing a tight-fitting gown covered in lace. In Princio's eyes, it looked like a room suited for a doll.

"Marian!" he called out, running forward and nearly tripping over his heavy feet.

She smiled brightly upon seeing him, feeling a rush of excitement in the belief that she wouldn't be trapped much longer. Pressing himself against the outside of the glass, Princio tried pushing forward.

"Marian? Are you alright? How did you get in there?" he asked quickly, studying the box she was trapped within.

Marian couldn't hear his voice and shook her head in

response.

"Marian? Can you hear me?"

"I can't. I can't..."

Marian touched her throat, hearing her own voice slowly fading away. She tried repeating her words, but was unable to finish her sentence. As she looked at him, eyes wide with fear, Princio understood immediately. The terror on her face horrified him.

"Marian!" He pushed himself against the glass, making it rattle.

He slammed his fists into it, but to no avail.

"I'll get you out! I will!"

Marian shook her head in response, sliding her hands closer to Princio's fists. Princio stopped pounding the glass, and instead rested his head against it. His heavy breaths rose and fell like waves. She was so close yet still far from his reach. He grunted, punching the glass one last time in frustration when he heard Marian tapping the glass gently with her nails. He looked at her, still unable to hear the words slipping from her lips. He could read the expression in her watery eyes. He had seen this look before.

"How touching."

Marian and Princio looked up to see Feletti, watching the show. He was sitting on top of an old bread stand, which still held the faint smell of wheat and parley.

"There's nothing you can do. She is where she belongs," Feletti said, smiling with contentment.

"Feletti! What happened to her? What did you do?!" Princio screamed.

"I brought her back home! She's where she belongs," Feletti replied, leaping from the stand. "And this is where she'll stay forever."

Princio ignored his words, looking for anything that could break the glass. He found part of an old chair and carried it over his shoulder, returning to the glass box.

"Back away! Back away!" he ordered.

Marian quickly backed away, seeing him lift the broken chair piece.

Feletti grinned. "I wouldn't do that," he warned.

Princio swung the chair into the glass, breaking the wood into several pieces without even making a dent. He growled, searching for something stronger. He found a pair of swords which had been used in the Cirque for swallowing tricks. But even with all of his strength, the weapons didn't make a scratch. The glass remained untouched.

"You can't break it. You can't free her. She's back home and that's where she'll stay." Feletti calmly explained.

Princio dropped the swords, tired from the constant swinging. In his peripheral vision, Feletti's smile grew wider and wider until it covered the width of his entire face. Without thinking, Princio threw one of the swords at him. Feletti lifted his arm and moved to the left, dodging the blade easily.

"This is not her home! Her home is with her brother!" Princio yelled.

"This is where she lived, until I gave her to that family," Feletti corrected.

Princio looked back at Marian with wide eyes. She stared back at him, wearing the same look of confusion.

"She didn't tell you?" Feletti looked at Marian, tilting his head and tutting in a amused yet disappointed tone. "Did you honestly forget?" he asked Marian mockingly.

She backed away from the glass in terror, crawling away from him to the very back of the room.

Princio moved towards Feletti and demanded, "Forget what?"

"Marian is a doll, Princio. A doll! When her father came crawling to me, begging for the daughter his wife always wanted, I gave her to him!" Boldly, Feletti pointed at her.

He leapt forward, jumping onto a tower of old crates with ease. He sat down, his legs spread out, using his hands to stay in place. He was seething, teetering on the brink of madness and refinement. His eyes were unable to look away from her as he remembered the first time he saw her. The first time she made him feel something other than emptiness.

"Out of all my dolls, she was the most beautiful. I didn't realize what a gift I had until she was gone. It pained me to give her away, but I made sure I'd have her once again, at the moment of my choosing. After all of these years... And I couldn't have picked a better time."

Princio placed his hands back on the glass causing Marian hesitantly to move toward him.

"I have so many dolls in my collection. But she was different. She was always different. But make no mistake my friend, she is a doll, through and through. She's already beginning to change. Her voice will die, and her skin will become pale and thick. She will remain inside this house, which is fit for the most precious of all dolls. My doll."

Marian pressed her hands and face against the glass, trying to say his name. "Prin...Princio... Princio," she barely whispered.

"There's nothing you can do to stop the process. She has, and always will be, just...a...doll. Just as you will always be a monstrous, grotesque, and unwanted prince."

Princio clenched his hair with his hands. His face turned red with anger. He began breathing so heavily that he was starting to become lightheaded.

"No! You pretended to be my friend! You were lying to me about my ugliness the whole time. You're the monster!" he cried.

Feletti chuckled in response, "And if I am..." He raised himself upward, lifting his face, clanking and snapping like refined wood. "What can you do about it?" he taunted.

Princio didn't respond, growling with anger.

Changing tactics Feletti asked, "You wanted a favor? I can grant it for you."

Princio didn't reply as his nostrils flared.

"You see, as your 'friend,' I wanted to deliver and brought you a gift." Reaching behind his back, he tugged at his collar and released a long cape. Holding it open, Princio watched, amazed as the fabric changed from a pale and coarse material to a darker color with a smooth texture. "If you want to see your parents again, Marian will remain a doll and live in my shop." The images of Princio's parents, the king and queen, appeared and flashed within the dark cape, alongside Marian. "If you want to save Marian from spending her eternity as a doll, then you will never see your parents again. It's that simple."

His heart sank. Princio desired to see his family again. He desired the relationship that life took away when he was so young.

"Do you want it?"

Princio watched as the images on his cape faded in and out, until he could no longer see his parents or Marian. Feletti dropped the cape, gently pulling it behind him as it swayed around his body.

"Do you want it, prince of Lucca?"

"How can you be so cruel?" Princio groaned, grinding his teeth.

"Cruel is all I know, and all that I am! Make your choice now!" Feletti screeched.

Princio looked at Marian, who shook her head several times.

"Let me go," she whispered.

Princio took his mask off and turned to Feletti, who was waiting for his answer.

"I'm going to choose another option." He threw his mask at Feletti who dodged it, but didn't move in time to avoid his sword swinging down. Princio sliced Feletti's hat in half. Falling backward, Feletti caught himself just before his legs broke. He crouched on the ground like a strange animal and stared up at Princio, slightly intrigued by the sudden attack.

"Nice swing. But you missed," Feletti taunted, smirking. He swung his arms around in circles, until clear strings flung forth from his fingers. He casted the strings outward, wrapping and binding Princio tightly like spider webs. The strings bound Princio so tightly that his clothing started to rip. Furious at the sight, Marian kicked her feet against the glass, trying to break free.

"You would rather die than just make a choice?!" Feletti yelled at him.

"I won't die, you will!" Princio responded. He kicked the fallen sword across the floor, snapping one of Feletti's legs. He fell harshly, lowering the strings in response. Princio freed himself from the bindings, tugging at the strings and dragging Feletti with great force. Feletti growled, feeling his leg break loose from his body. He grabbed the closest thing to hold onto. Raising one of his arms, Feletti sent Princio soaring across the room and into the blue lock of the carousel. The impact left Princio feeling stunned and dizzy. He barely saw Feletti getting back up, fixing his leg with ease. As he drifted in and out of consciousness, he watched, realizing that Feletti's entire body was made of wood. Several parts of his face were cracked and splintered, and strands of his hair were scattered across the marble floor.

'He's a doll himself!' Princio concluded in horror.

With his leg snapped back in place, Feletti retrieved his arm, connecting it properly under his shoulder. He pulled and snapped the dead strings from his flexible hands with ease.

"You can't kill me Princio. No matter how much you break me down I can still be repaired. It's the perfect form, wouldn't you agree?"

Princio pulled himself up, his head pounding as he struggled to turn the giant key. After spitting some blood from his lips, he forced himself onto the carousel, which was just beginning to move. The lights slowly turned on and the repetitive, childlike music began to flow. Feletti jumped onto the carousel, following Princio as it began to spin around. Feletti lost sight of Princio momentarily, who was hiding on the floor of a swan shaped seat. With every clicking and clacking step, Feletti peered around the carousel stalking his friend.

"Come now, Princio. Hiding are we?"

Princio waited, stilling his breathing.

"I suppose I owe your parents for this form. If they weren't such wasteful, ungrateful and spoiled rulers than I would have never been able to live again. I'd still be less than my former self, lurking in the shadows."

He passed each horse, watching them move up and down, anticipating Princio's attack. Feletti paused over the seat which Princio was hiding under. Taking his chance, Princio leapt out and threw his long blanket over Feletti. His flimsy feet crossed over each other until he tripped over the edge of the rotating ride. Princio grabbed Feletti and threw him into the center of the ride. In a rage he ripped through the blanket and then his coat. Desperately, he grabbed the bottom of the nearest golden pole attached to the floor. Growling loudly, he felt his body being pulled into the center of the ride. He couldn't fight it. Princio clasped his arms around a nearby horse, watching Feletti struggle to pick himself back up. From his legs, pieces of string became trapped under the wooden floor, caught in continuous turns. Feletti felt a violent tug, as each turn threatened to pull him under. He fought against the carousel's pull, struggling to keep his grip. As he slowly lost his grip on the golden pole, Feletti laughed.

"Even if you are handsome, you'll never believe it. I'll be back. I can't die, I'm made of wood! I can always repair myself! When I do, there will be no punishment severe enough for the likes of you!" His wooden hands finally snapped from the pressure. Feletti was flung over the side, spinning around with the ride. His legs were crushed into the carousel gears, which pulled him in. Feletti let out one last, desperate yell as the gears smashed him. The ride was brought to a slow crawl, before finally stopping altogether.

Chapter Fourteen

Freedom

Princio fell to his knees panting. He barely had a second to compose himself when the sound of glass shattering startled him. He looked up and saw Marian on the ground. She was surrounded by broken glass and the dismantled furniture she had used to break free. Princio limped towards her, fearing what condition he would find her in. Would she still be the Marian he had grown to love? He gently picked her up into his arms. With relief he saw that her pale and stiff body had become rosy and soft once again. Marian remained unresponsive, but only for a moment. Her chest rose and fell as she let out a heavy breath of relief upon seeing that Princio was holding her. She smiled brightly, embracing him tightly and whispering his name. His warmth engulfed her as she felt safe for the first time in her life. Each time she repeated his name with relief and love, Princio held her a little tighter, worried that if he let go she would vanish. As much as Princio would love to hold Marian forever, he had one very important task he needed to do. The sooner he did so, the better for them and the kingdom.

Princio grunted several times, tugging and pulling the pole out from the wooden floor of the carousel. Marian watched quietly as he roughly grabbed the diseased, disfigured horse, ripping it from its space in the far back of the ride. Feletti had come to Lucca imprisoned in this horse. Feletti was gone now, and soon so would be his prison. He felt the warmth of the fire on his skin as he lugged the horse to the roaring fireplace. With a grunt, he heaved the decayed horse into it. The color of the fire changed briefly, as the black and dark blue flames blended into the red and yellow blaze. The massive flames cast shadows across walls of the annexed building. Princio and Marian watched the horse burn in silence, until it was nothing but ashes. Marian's slender hand reached for Princio. Surprising him, she laced her fingers with his, reassuring him she would never leave. By destroying the horse Feletti had come from, they both hoped he would be destroyed for good.

"Yes, you're made of wood. And wood burns." Princio spat at the fire.

Epilogue

"Princio, Princio…"

He groaned, hearing his name in the distance. Trying to ignore the voice calling out to him, Princio turned over to the other side of his bed, burying his face underneath one of four pillows. His left leg kicked out from under his blankets as he tried to find a new comfortable position.

"Princio! Princio!"

The voice grew louder and louder until…

"Princio! Get up! Wake up!" Marian called running into his room with reckless abandon, flinging his bedroom door open.

"I'm up, I'm…" he trailed off, drifting back into sleep.

"C'mon, get up!" Marian yelled, jumping onto his bed wildly.

She landed on his legs and looked at Princio, who was trying to hide under his pillow. He let out a soft yelp from the jump, instantly awake and aware. He winced, draping one arm across his forehead before looking at Marian, who was smiling down at him with delight.

"Marian? What's going on?" he asked, his voice muffled.

"It's snowing! Come! You must see!" she cried joyously.

"Snow? It hasn't snowed in Lucca…for at least ten years right?" He yawned trying to process what was happening.

"Come!"

"I am. Just five more…" Princio's voice trailed off again. He leaned back onto his nearest pillow, before Marian slowly bent down and gave him a delicate kiss on his lips.

"Your highness, it's snowing. You must wake up and see this sight. It may never snow again in our lifetime," Marian said with a soothing voice.

Princio smiled, opening his eyes and seeing her clearly for the first time. Her blue eyes sparkled unlike he had ever seen before. Her long hair cascaded down both of her shoulders. The natural light from the white sky created a glow around her. She looked like an angel. And he felt like the luckiest man in the world.

"I'm up now."

Marian smiled, holding out her hand for him to take. He slowly and delicately grasped hers, treasuring her touch like the timeless woman she was.

Princio, the forgotten prince, finally discovered the truth that had been hidden from him all his life. He was not a hideous monster, but was actually a handsome prince all along. However, Princio had no intention of reclaiming his throne, or of ever hiding alone again. He decided to share his new life with Marian, a young woman who he never saw as a doll, but as the young woman he grew to love. Lucca was wiped clean again with the snow, as though the land was reborn. The evil presence in the kingdom had burned to ashes, banished forever.

Princio never revealed himself to Lucca as their prince. However, he still hoped Marian would be his queen, even in secret. Perhaps Marian denied all others but her heart always knew she would find Princio. After their wedding, Marian and Princio made the palace their home, unbeknownst to the people of Lucca.

Placido and Princio became close friends once Princio returned his sister home. Placido finally learned of their courtship and taught Princio the toymaking craft. With his help, Placido's toy shop became famous around the country. Orders wouldn't stop coming in as children and couples practically begged for the most unique and coveted toys. The success was more than Placido could have asked for. Soon after, he met and fell in love with a woman from the kingdom. They married and built a family of their own, holding true to the values that were instilled upon them by their families. It wouldn't be long until Princio and Marian would know the same blessings, having several children and a future that seemed limitless. Growing up and growing older together, Marian and Princio were inseparable, still reliving the innocence of childhood while riding the carousel that brought them together.

Jennifer Renson-Chiappetta's passion for writing began in childhood. Her writing career spanned from articles in Lost Treasure Magazine to her self published poetry books; *Delightfully Dark: A Collection of Poems and Tales*, *Eo: Go, walk, ride, sail, pass, travel* and *Uncharted*. Presently she is a mother and wife; she enjoys spending her time with her family and friends, writing, crafting, specifically cross-stitching and reveling in Victorian Era ambiances while living in New Jersey.

www.ingramcontent.com/pod-product-compliance
Lightning Source LLC
Chambersburg PA
CBHW020659120726
47906CB00001B/337